A BOY'S TAIL

MARK ROGERS

A BOY'S TAIL

iUniverse books may be ordered through booksellers or by contacting:

iUniverse
1663 Liberty Drive
Bloomington, IN 47403
www.iuniverse.com
844-349-9409

Because of the dynamic nature of the internet, any web addresses or links contained in this book may have changed since publication and may no longer be valid. The views expressed in this work are solely those of the author and do not necessarily reflect the views of the publisher, and the publisher hereby disclaims any responsibility for them.

Any people depicted in stock imagery provided by Getty Images are models, and such images are being used for illustrative purposes only. Certain stock imagery © Getty Images.

ISBN: 978-1-6632-3798-9 (sc)
ISBN: 978-1-6632-3797-2 (e)

Library of Congress Control Number: 2022906849

Print information available on the last page.

iUniverse rev. date: 05/13/2022

DEDICATION

When I first started working with the Trevor Project, it was in a kind of "Dear Abby"–type program called "Ask Trevor." I would browse through letters and answer as many as I wanted. I would refer the suicidal ones to the administrators for more professional help. The very first suicidal one I found was from a Jon M. from Nashville. He went into great detail describing his life and the reason for his attempt to kill himself. In a word, religion.

Less than a year after Jon M.'s letter to Trevor, Chris C., a kid from my hometown, hung himself at the age of sixteen. I never knew Chris, but I was told that he was well liked, wasn't bullied, and was into sports. He had everything to live for, yet to my knowledge, he took the reason for taking his life with him to the grave. In pictures of him in his high school yearbook and obituary, the sadness and pain in his eyes are haunting.

What struck me so was that all the information I could find about Chris C.'s life so accurately mirrored Jon M.'s life. I was horrified. I suspected that the only reason he had for committing suicide was because, as puberty erupted inside him, he was discovering that he had an attraction to other boys, and his parents were highly religious.

Countless times since then I have seen similar scenarios play out in my work with the Trevor Project. Some are bullied unmercifully, while others have deeply religious parents. But none deserve to be forced into thinking that their only option is to end their lives. While you do your best to help these kids, even if your efforts are successful, you seldom hear back from them. But Jon M.

survived his attempt and reached out to Trevor for help. I hope he is still alive and doing well. But much to my sorrow, Chris C. did not, and I can only wish that he had. It is to Chris that I dedicate this effort.

CONTENTS

ACKNOWLEDGMENT

All notes referenced in this book are directly quoted and sourced from online articles and publications by various authors for the Trevor Project and other sources.

INTRODUCTION

This story was written in order to illustrate to those who use religion to denounce others of the damage they can do with their religious declarations. Thus I set it in a sci-fi setting where the dominant species has evolved from horses instead of primates. Instead of facial hair that male humans begin growing at the onset of puberty, the males of this world begin to grow a tail. This world is governed by a one-world theocratic government, and the people, being of several breeds of horses, accept one another with no prejudices, except for one that has come from misguided religious interpretations. And our main character is about to find out what happens to him.

In this world, our tail begins.

CHAPTER 1

Personal Discovery

Tyler

Tyler Palomino felt that he was just an average midteen stud horse. Just as a human pubescent boy awaits the day his facial hair begins to grow out, he'd been waiting for the appearance of his horse-person tail hair. Yet despite being a tailless late bloomer at fifteen, his filly classmates still considered him to be handsome, athletic, and colt-like cute.

But now, finally, the day had come. His anxiously awaited tail began to grow out. That morning he awoke to an unusual itching across his tailbone. Reaching down to scratch, his fingers touched the first signs of hair starting to grow out. That startled him fully awake.

He quickly got out of bed, backed up to the full-length mirror that hung on his closet door, and revealed his tailbone area. There was the unmistakable beginnings of a patch of hair extending across his tailbone and filling the valley between his buttock muscles. He was finally going to get his adult tail. But then his moment of joy quickly turned to horror as the hair was unmistakably brown instead of white. His secret attraction only to other males would be found out if anyone else ever saw his brown tail hair. It would be better to have a tail come in late than to be brown.

Religious leaders taught that any stud who grew a brown tail did so as a willful choice and an unnatural act of defiance against the Great One. They were to be despised as outcasts. And Ty believed it. That is, until the day he discovered his own brown tail hair.

Ty dressed himself enough to get into the bathroom without anyone seeing his discovery and quickly found a razor. He held it as the thought of using it to kill himself swirled in his mind. It seemed like an eternity as he contemplated the very real option of suicide. That way his parents wouldn't have to bear the ridicule they would surely face from all their friends in church. The temptation was great, and his hand trembled as he held the razor blade over his wrists.

No! He could not do it. His gentle nature would not let him. Suicide was a permanent solution to a temporary problem. It would be easier to shave off the hair for now and deal with the problem later. So he shaved off all the newly grown hair on his tailbone. He then carefully cleaned the razor and washed everything down the drain, making sure all evidence of the brown hair was gone.

As a colt, Ty had always been very faithful to the world religion. He never wanted to defy the Great One and grow a brown tail, but there it was. And every day he was going to have to make sure he shaved that area clean and disposed of any evidence in the razor or washbasin. It would take only one incident of not shaving off every brown hair from his tailbone, and he would be found out in the gym class shower. Even the insinuation of any stud growing a brown tail was enough to bring down all of society's ridicule and hatred against him.

Though the religious community had preached against their evil sinfulness, as no decent horse-person would want to grow a brown tail, there always seemed to be a small minority of studs who had willfully grown one. Why anyone would choose to grow a brown tail knowing full well the nasty treatment he would undoubtedly receive as a result was illogical. It had always puzzled Ty. It was something he certainly did not want to experience himself. He had heard the ridicule and nasty comments. He had even heard of some studs being assaulted and beaten just for having a brown tail. So Ty had to keep his tail a secret. His parents were very religious, and the thought of what they might do scared him. He was sure that his same-sex attraction was not a willful decision. It was obvious to him: He was born that way.

It was a secret that he knew he could keep hidden for only just so long. He knew deep down that day he would be exposed would eventually come. But it came sooner than he expected.

Ironically, when he got to school that morning, the entire school was buzzing with the latest news. Ty quickly overheard two fillies talking about what had happened the previous evening.

"And he was found hanging in his bedroom closet. Needless to say, his mom was horrified when she found him," one filly said.

The other replied, "I heard there was a suicide note, and he was so sorry that he was a brown-tail."

"Who was that?" Ty asked.

"It was Jamie Colter," answered one on the fillies.

"Oh God, no! Not Jamie!" Ty exclaimed. "I know him. He was on my ball team and was really good. I can't believe he'd kill himself."

Another stud joined the conversation. "I would have never known he was a brown-tail. But then, he always was a private person. And come to think of it, pretty guarded about taking a shower with the rest of us studs. Maybe that's why."

Ty was beside himself as his own secret pressed against the back of his mind. *Is that my fate?* he wondered. No, he didn't want to off himself. There must be a better way. It was something he would ponder for the rest of the school term, until summer break.

CHAPTER 2

Day of Reckoning

Jamie Colter's suicide never left Ty's mind. On the morning of the last day of school, those thoughts had distracted him as he shaved off his tail hair. He knew it was the last time he'd have to shave for a while, and he hurried to finish. When he came home that afternoon, he found his parents in distress. And his world all came apart on him.

"Tyler, into the den. Now!" bellowed his dad. When Ty closed the door behind him, he saw his dad holding some brown hair. Ty had failed to fully dispose of the evidence that morning.

"What do you make of this?" his dad demanded. Ty didn't know what to say. "How dare you be so sinful as to grow a brown-tail? Haven't we raised you right?"

Ty's mom choked out, "Please change your ways!" She was now in tears, while his dad continued to berate him for choosing to be so sinful. "Change your ways, so your tail will grow out white!" he demanded.

By now, Ty himself was almost in tears himself. "I can't help it. Try as I may, I have no attraction to any fillies, just studs."

With that, his dad grabbed him by his horse collar and dragged him to the front door. He opened it and then reached around back, grabbed the middle of Ty's belt, picked him up, and heaved him out the door. Ty flew across the front porch, barely missing the stone walk, landing in the grass with a thud. "You're no son of mine. Don't

5

you ever come back here again!" his dad yelled at him, then slammed the door shut.

So there he was, thrown out of his home with nothing but the clothes on his back. And he had no money in his pocket. Luckily Ty found a place to sleep that night but had nothing to eat the next day. It was summer break, so thankfully he didn't have to go to school. By evening, Ty was quite hungry. The next day, he knew that he had to find a way of getting something to eat. That would mean either dumpster diving or getting some money somehow.

He wasn't the type to steal. But as luck would have it, a different opportunity arose unexpectedly. Ty found himself in a cruising area and was quickly picked up by an older brown-tail stallion. He pulled up in a car and lowered the passenger-side window. Ty was about to learn about "survival sex" by being forced into hustling.

"Hey, young brown-tail, you available?" the stallion asked.

Ty didn't know exactly what to say except, "What do you mean?"

"You want to make some money?"

"Yeah," Ty said sheepishly.

"Then hop in." Ty did as he was told and stepped into the car. The stallion took him to a secluded spot and parked.

Ty was a bit scared, and the stallion saw that. "I won't hurt you. I promise." What the stallion then did to him was unspeakable. But Ty was stuck without any alternative. It was the only way he could get some money to survive.

After this horrible experience, the stallion drove him back to where they first met and dropped him off at the curb. "You're one hot, young stud, kid. See you in a few days. Same place?" the stallion asked as he handed Ty a wad of money. Ty nodded to him as the stallion drove off. Ty looked at the wad of money. It was enough to get him a room for one night and something to fill his hungry belly.

But then Ty realized he'd have to do it again tomorrow if he wanted to survive. He'd have to act like nothing happened, then go to the cruise area, and do *it* all over again. It was just like the stallion had said. This was something he'd have to get used to doing. Every day. From now on. Just to survive.

CHAPTER 3

Survival

When Tyler awoke the next morning, he knew what he had to do that day. So he got dressed, checked out of the hotel, and headed for the cruise area. He was scared of what he would have to do to get some money, but he knew he had to do whatever it took. And he was going to have to do it again the next day, and the day after that, and for however long it took until he could figure out a better way of living. It was survival sex or starve.

Ty didn't like having to sell himself or having to take whatever somebody wanted to do to him. But what choice did he have? At his age and without a parental permission slip, he couldn't get any kind of a real job. And all because he was a brown-tail. *Why me?* kept running through his mind. *What did I do to deserve being a brown-tail?* He had no answer. No extra clothes either. He had no home, no food, and no way of getting any of it without either selling himself or resorting to becoming a thief. Ty was too honest of a young stud to resort to that.

So when Ty got to a wall in the cruise area, he took the hustler's stance. He leaned up against the wall and pulled his right hoof up and just under his butt to show off his package to oncoming traffic.

His first pickup of the day pulled up and lowered the passenger window. Ty cautiously approached the car door and saw a nice-looking elderly stallion at the wheel. "You available?"

Ty opened the door and climbed in. Once seated, they drove

off to whatever would happen. This time it was just light sex. After it was all over, the stallion thanked him. "You did well," he told Ty. Then he handed Ty some money. "That's all I have." Ty knew that was no doubt a little white lie, but it was enough for him to accept. The stallion then drove back to the cruise area and dropped him off.

Ty thought, *That wasn't so bad. I can handle that.* The money the stallion gave him wasn't much. It certainly wouldn't cover what he knew he would need for the day's food and hotel expenses, let alone get some much-needed clothes. But as he soon found out, it was the going rate for what he had done. And he quickly found out that he didn't have any choice in the matter. His customers would decide for him, and he was just going to have to let them do whatever they wanted to do to him or starve. He chose not to starve that day or every day thereafter. As if he had any choice at all.

Sometimes he had to spend all day and into the evening before making enough money to get through to the next day. On many days, there were too few customers for him to even have a decent meal. But on occasion, one of his clients would be generous and give him a "bonus" amount. It was during those times that he quickly learned how to manage his money. He also had to learn the ropes of the hustling trade, and learn them quickly.

He also had to dodge the Morality Police, one of the theocracy's agencies that periodically raided the cruise areas and conducted sting operations. Thanks to several other hustlers who befriended him, Ty was not caught. Mind you, they were not that friendly as they were competing for the same clients, but they knew all too well what would happen to Ty should he be arrested.

The Morality Police had the authority to arrest any brown-tails selling themselves in any way. And in the case of minors like

Tyler, they would send him off to Correction Camp. That meant an endless incarceration consisting of torture, beatings, mind manipulation, and "rumored" treatments that many of the more experienced hustlers were most familiar with having been victims of the theocratic system of rule.

One of them, going only by his assumed first name—as was the practice with many hustlers—of Davie, was the first to warn Tyler away from his first encounter with a sting operation officer. Ty found out that Davie had been through it all. His parents had thrown him out of his home when he was just fourteen. Davie's mom had accidentally seen him in the shower. She had seen the first brown tail hairs even before he realized they were beginning to come out. As with Tyler, Davie was berated by his parents, putting him out on the street with nothing but the clothes on his back.

"I had just turned fourteen and was naive and gullible," Davie told Ty. "That made me easy prey for the Morality Police to catch in a sting operation. I can't remember just how long it was, something like maybe four or five years, of being constantly mentally harassed, physically tortured, and abused. All of this with the official aim of forcing me to 'straighten out' my sexual attractions." And it's not that Davie didn't try. He just could not change, no matter what. The feelings simply came from so deep within him that he couldn't help it. So when he saw that Tyler was new to the street and couldn't tell a sting officer from a real client, he couldn't bear to see him end up at Correction Camp like he had. It was then that he and several other hustlers educated Tyler on realities of the trade.

Even though Davie befriended Tyler, he still kept their friendship at a distance. That's because Correction Camp staff often extorted from their charges the names of other brown-tail minors. Then they would find and arrest them for no other reason. A couple of other hustlers who helped educate Tyler had been picked up under just such circumstances. One was arrested in the middle of the school day. He was dragged out of class, humiliated, and bawling like a newborn foal. The rest of the hustlers helped each other when it came to the Morality Police, even if they were rather independent otherwise.

And that was how Ty managed to survive the summer months, spending much of each day servicing whoever came by wanting Ty's body for sex. And just like the first stallion had said, he got used to being treated like a mare. He knew that to survive, he was going to have to live like that, at least until he got older.

CHAPTER 4

Found Out

It started out just like every other day after selling himself the night before, so he could have some money for something to eat and, if he were lucky, a place to bed down for the night. It was a challenge just to get through the day somehow without anyone finding out that his parents threw him out on the street with nothing but the clothes on his back. All summer long, Ty had nothing to shave with, so his tail had grown to almost a foot long. But he was determined to go back to school like normal that fall. The day school started, he didn't have gym class until last period. But he still had to be cautious in dressing for it, or his tail would be seen.

Fortunately, the class was just light exercise and didn't require showering at the end. But he had to hide what he knew would certainly show—his brown-tail hair growth. He succeeded during most of the class. As he dressed at the end of the period, his best friend, Kyle Whitehorse, sat on the bench beside him. He looked at Ty and suddenly froze. Kyle's eyes got big and his jaw dropped as a look of horror spread across on his face. Ty just as suddenly realized what Kyle saw. A feeling of dread engulfed Ty as he hurriedly covered his backside.

"Ty," Kyle whispered to him, "is that what I think it is?"

Tyler whispered back, almost whimpering, "Please don't say anything."

"Ty, of course I won't say anything. But we need to talk."

"OK, but somewhere private."

"Of course. Come with me."

Now both fully dressed, Kyle stood up and led Ty out of the locker room to the now-silent equipment room. He shut the door behind them.

"Kyle, I swear I didn't choose this—"

Kyle cut him off. "Ty, you're my best bud. I've known you since first grade. I don't think you would choose it. The religious leaders aren't supposed to be wrong, and they say it's a choice. But to be honest, I'm skeptical."

"That's just it. I didn't want to be different. But I've come to realize I am, and it's showing." Tyler explained everything that had happened to him that fateful day.

"Here I was, beginning to think you were a late bloomer. But if they threw you out that long ago, where have you been? Where have you been sleeping?"

"The first night I found a big box behind a store and curled up in it. But I've had to sell myself on the street every night since. I feel terrible." Tears streamed down Ty's cheeks.

"My gawd, Ty, that's awful! You can't go on like that, bro. Why didn't you tell me?"

"I was so ashamed. I didn't know who I could trust."

"You know you can trust me. I promise I won't tell anyone. But what are you going to do? Has anybody else found out?"

"No. But I don't know if I can take it much longer. I feel so worthless."

"Look, maybe I can get my folks to put you up for a while. We might have to think of something to tell them. But they're pretty open-minded, so you might be able to tell them the truth."

"I don't know. But anything is better than what I've had to do ever since." Ty began to cry uncontrollably.

Kyle wrapped his arms around Tyler and comforted him. For the first time since his parents found out, Ty felt wanted and protected. They left school and went to Kyle's house. There, in tears, Tyler opened up to Kyle's parents. They were moved, and shocked. Kyle's mother sat there in silence, wiping one tear after another from her eyes. His dad just stood there with a look of sorrow and compassion on his face.

"Of course, you can stay here," Kyle's dad stated. "We can't let you spend another night out on the street."

"And we certainly can't have you selling yourself just to have something to eat, let alone a place to stay," his mom remarked. "So that settles it. But you will have to sleep in the spare stall though."

"You don't think I'd try something with Kyle, do you? We've known each other since first grade, and he's more like a brother to me. I wouldn't—"

"Of course, we trust you, Tyler," Kyle's dad interrupted. "You've always been an honest colt. Maybe too honest for your own good at times."

CHAPTER 5

Recollections and Then Reality

Kyle suggested that Tyler take a shower before heading for bed. It was music to Ty's ears. They went into the bathroom, and Ty started stripping down. "I'll wash your clothes while you shower," Kyle offered. Ty slipped into the shower and turned on the water as Kyle gathered up the clothing and headed for the laundry room downstairs.

As the warm water streamed down Tyler's muscular young body, his mind drifted to what he had been through the last few months. Bad memories still fresh in his mind seemed to wash away like the soapsuds that were streaming down the velvet hair on his skin. He finally felt safe and let go of all the abuse he'd experienced. Sure, some of the stallions had given him some nice compliments. But instead of making him feel good about himself, those compliments made him feel used and dirty.

Ty lathered up his mane with shampoo as the water ran down his chest. Then he reached back and ran the lather down his ever-lengthening tail. It was the feeling of maturity he had often yearned for—before his parents threw him out. For a while after, it had given him a feeling of shame. But now he was becoming more comfortable with his growing sexual identity. He turned around, leaned his head back, and let the water rinse the suds from his mane, run down his back, and rinse his tail. His tail now gave him a boost of assurance to his masculinity.

Sure, Ty still felt an attraction to other stallions. Mares were, well, nice friends. But oh, how beautiful were stallions in Tyler's mind. How their rippling muscles moved, and bulges in just the right places. Their masculine faces, flowing tails, and overall masculine looks. All made Ty's hormones race full throttle. Certainly he could find a brown-tail stud who would love him as much as he wanted to love another stud. Wasn't love all about caring for each other? What difference would it make whether the horse he loved was a stallion or a mare? The religious writings had to be wrong. They preached love, but how could they say that loving someone of the same sex was wrong? How could love—any love—be wrong? It didn't make any sense to Tyler. Besides, those writings were thousands of years old, before all the scientific knowledge of today. Heck, they thought the world was flat back then. If they were wrong about that, certainly they could be wrong about loving another stud. Just like they had to be wrong about tail color being a choice. Ty knew he didn't choose to have a brown tail, just like he didn't choose to be attracted to other studs.

"Ty, your clothes are going to be dry before you are!"

Tyler was suddenly brought back to reality. "I'm almost done." But what to put on? Kyle had taken the few clothes he had to the laundry.

Just then Kyle cracked the door just enough to hand in a robe and briefs. At least Ty wouldn't have to wrap a towel around himself just to be presentable. Slipping on a clean robe would almost feel luxurious. And the briefs even had a tail opening. They were the first tail briefs he had ever put on. He just had to check in the mirror to see how he looked with his brown tail hanging free out back. And although his tail was nowhere near the length of an adult tail, it was the first time he actually felt good about himself. He even felt proud of his tail. Like a real stallion. Pulling the robe around himself and tying the belt, he confidently opened the bathroom door.

"Man, I thought you had drowned in there," Kyle remarked.

"Just getting cleaned off," Ty shot back. "After what I've been through, I thought I'd never get clean again."

"You feel better now?"

"Yeah. You have no idea." Kyle only smiled back.

To Tyler, the bed in the spare stall looked like a refuge from his troubles. It even felt like one, all soft and comfy. He bedded down, and no sooner had he pulled the covers up than sleep overtook him. He was safe.

CHAPTER 6

Morning Comes

"Tyler!" He awoke with a start. "You'll be late for school," the voice yelled. Sitting up in bed, he looked around and saw his clothes neatly folded on the dresser. But on top was a clean set of clothes he had not seen before.

Kyle knocked at the door. "Ty, you up yet?"

Ty answered, "Come on in, Kyle."

Kyle saw Ty standing at the dresser, holding up a new pair of tail jeans. Looking over at Kyle, Ty's expression said it all. "I thought you'd like a pair of new jeans, since you're past the bobtail stage. I got them for myself just the other day, but I think you need them more."

"But I can't show my tail in public," Ty said as his eyes began to tear up.

"Well, maybe not right today. But at least around here on the weekends you can."

"Oh, Kyle, you're such a good friend." Ty threw his arms around Kyle and hugged him.

"You need to get dressed if you want to make it to school on time. At least you don't have gym today," said Kyle. The two held each other in their arms.

"Yes. And thanks so much for the tail briefs. They're the first pair I've ever had."

"I figured you were ready for them. And you do look good in them, Ty. I knew you would. Now all we need to do is get you in touch with the local brown-tail community."

"But I've been to the cruise area for the last few months!"

"No, no, not that part. I mean the *real* community. And not the underground bars either. Besides, they wouldn't let a minor in anyway. I'm talking about a secret social network that I found last night while you slept. It's buried in the internet, hidden from interference by the theocrats. Its members are all ages, working to bring the truth to the public. Some are scientists who now claim there's enough proof that being a brown-tail is not a choice. That you were born that way. But the theocrats dispute them and call them heretics. They argue that it's the religion that's messed up, and they can prove it. I think they're right, and so do a lot of other people. After all, if science proves that being a brown-tail is not a choice, their whole idea of it being a sin falls apart. I think the theocrats simply don't want their religion to lose the power."

"Wow, that's fantastic! And you found that all because of me?"

"Hey, you're my best bud, like I said. And what are friends for?"

Ty hugged Kyle again. "Now get dressed. I'll see you downstairs."

At breakfast, Kyle's mom served up Ty's favorite: hot oatmeal with cinnamon sugar. To Ty, it was a banquet after spending much of the time while on the street having to dumpster dive for whatever he could find that was still edible. Some of what was found was so disgusting that it took all he could muster in order to eat, in order to keep from starving. But even just fresh oatmeal would have tasted so good to Ty.

"My, you practically inhaled that bowl," Kyle's mom remarked. "Good thing I made extra. Care for some more?"

"Oh, yes. Thank you! You don't know just how good this tastes to me," Ty said between mouthfuls of oatmeal.

All Kyle could do was grin.

CHAPTER 7

A Troubling Beginning

At school that morning, Tyler and Kyle joined the rest of the students going to class. One was Kurt Clydesdale, the local preacher's son. He was just about as religious as his folks. Kurt, also known as "Casey" or "KC" (for his initials) noticed that Tyler was about the only stud still not wearing his tail out of his jeans. He called out, "Hey, Ty, how come you aren't showing any tail yet? You certainly aren't that late a bloomer, are you? Or are you trying to hide something?"

"What do you mean?" Ty asked.

But by that time, KC had him by the back of the jeans. "Let's see what you're hiding," he said as he grabbed the back of Ty's shirt and began to pull down on his jeans and up on his shirt.

About then Kyle grabbed KC's wrists and stopped him. "Leave him alone, KC, or you'll have to answer to me."

Both studs were heavy into sports and knew they were an even match for each other. So KC released Ty's clothing. "It's his right as to whether he wants to show any tail or not," Kyle told him. "Now mind your own business."

"But it *is* the Great One's business, and the Great One expects me to do His work," KC insisted.

"So let's see your license. Or is it too hard to carry around those stone tablets?" Kyle mocked him in return. "The Great One didn't give you the right to rip the clothes off someone just because they aren't showing any tail."

"You just wait, pony boy. I'm going to find out what you're hiding," KC threatened before walking away.

Just as KC disappeared into the crowd, Joey Quarterhorse came up to them. "I saw what KC did to you. He tried to do the same thing to me yesterday, but the science teacher stopped him. I've been scared of him ever since."

Noticing that Joey wasn't showing any tail either, Ty whispered to him, "Are you one too?"

Surprised, Joey asked "You mean—"

"Yeah," Ty interrupted him. Ty, Kyle, and Joey went off to a corner by themselves. "So just how much tail do you have, Joey?"

"Actually, I'm almost fully grown," he whispered. "But I've been hiding it for almost a year. It would be quite a challenge, what with gym. But I got a disability exemption from my doctor and got out of it last year."

"I don't think I could manage that. I'm an athlete, and that would look strange."

"So what have you been doing?" Joey asked.

"My tail didn't start coming in until late last school year, so I was shaving it off. But then the last day of school, I got careless, and …" Ty began to tear up.

"Oh no. What happened, Ty?"

"My folks found out and threw me out in the street."

"Oh no! How awful."

"I don't want to talk about it." Ty was in tears now.

"I just found out yesterday," Kyle said. "So I got him to talk to my parents, and we took him in."

"I always thought you were a nice guy, Kyle," Joey said. "You've got a heart of gold."

Blushing, Kyle suddenly realized they needed to get to class. "Hey, we've got to get going. See you at lunch?"

"Yeah," the others said together. And each took off for their respective classes.

CHAPTER 8

New Friends

The studs managed to find one another in the middle of the lunchroom mayhem and sat at a table off by themselves. Tyler and Joey seemed to have a bond they hadn't had before. They couldn't help smiling at each another.

Kyle noticed and remarked, "Looks like you two found something in common."

"I think we have." Looking at Joey, Ty said, "Until now, I only thought of you as just another classmate, Joey. But I have always admired your artistic talent."

"Joey, you really are quite good with that stuff," Kyle remarked.

"Well, I always thought how great it must be to be athletic, like both you guys."

"Thanks, Joey," Ty said, Kyle nodding in agreement. "So do your parents know about you?"

"Actually, yes. They weren't too happy at first, but they aren't that religious. They are open-minded, so they came around pretty quickly. Now they are behind me, and I can be myself with them. They even got me tail pants to wear around the house. Sorry your folks reacted so badly, Ty."

"I'm just thankful for friends like Kyle. And that he has such understanding parents."

Kyle added, "I think knowing Ty since we were in first grade and that we've always been such good friends seemed to make a difference. They always did see others as being the same as themselves."

"Oh, just so you know, Kyle found some stuff about our kind on the net last night. Would you know anything about it that we don't?" Ty asked.

"Well, maybe. I know about a local underground group that gets together periodically to talk about religion, politics, and what we can do to change society's viewpoint, particularly the attitude of the religious establishment. I've been to a couple of meetings. Some feel that the scriptures are being misinterpreted, that they really don't condemn us or think we're hopeless sinners. I think they're right."

"That would be good news indeed," replied Ty. "But why would the religious leaders hold on to misinterpretations? Don't the rest of the scriptures preach love?"

"Yes, but the thought is that to remain in power, the hierarchy needs to have a whipping mule, and we're it. It's why they claim the scientists are heretics. Their whole power structure would collapse if they ever admitted they were wrong and that we're just a normal variation. So they twist around a couple of verses that kinda mention studs that did some horrible things to each other to make them say what they want them to say. They seem to paper over the Great Commandment that we should all love and care for each other."

"The religious leaders are such hypocrites," a voice behind them said. It was one of Kyle's friends, Andy Thoroughbred, and his mare friend Jennifer Trotter. The two had been inseparable since they were in fifth grade and obviously headed for the halter together after they graduated. "Mind if we join you?" Andy asked. They were welcomed by the studs. "We couldn't help seeing Kyle over here with you two, so we decided to see if you'd mind some more company."

"We heard what Joey said, and we both feel the same way," Jennifer remarked.

"Yeah. And we saw the incident with Joey and KC yesterday. We were about to step in, but the teacher beat us to it. I just can't stand what some of those religious types do to others."

"Andy, did you and Jennifer hear anything else?" Ty asked.

"What, about you and Joey? No, but I'm kinda thinking that there's something more than meets the eye here. Am I right?"

"Well, it depends on how open-minded you two are," Kyle injected.

"Hey, we're OK with brown-tails, if that's what you two are." Ty and Joey, both wide-eyed by now, slowly nodded. "That's cool. So you're now out with us. OK?" Ty and Joey just grinned.

"Not all white-tails look down on brown-tails," Kyle said.

"And you two make such a cute couple," Jennifer added.

Ty and Joey looked at each other and blushed. But it was something they all could agree on.

CHAPTER 9

Wet Dreams

Tyler managed to avoid running into KC for the rest of the day. And as he bedded down for the night, his thoughts turned to Joey. He'd never really given much thought to the little colt until then. Joey always seemed to be off doing his own thing, being in art class, active in the theater, drama classes, all the artistic stuff. And he was smart too. But Ty was more of the stud horse, active in all the sports young studs were usually involved in. But now he started to see something in Joey he had never seen before. Ty was attracted to this artsy little stud. Previously he had admired the athletic studs in his gym class, those with the rippling muscles, brawny good looks, and, oh, that masculine saunter in their gaits.

Joey was, well, different. Sure, he was colt-like cute. He was small for his age, almost like a pony instead of a stallion. He was not much for athletics, and not very coordinated in sports. Only the brawny stallions got into athletics, the muscular Clydesdales being the top studs. Joey was obviously no match for any of them. In gym class, Joey was always bested by the studs, and sometimes in the most humiliating fashion. Tyler often felt sorry for him.

What Tyler didn't know was that Joey's mother was a Lipizzaner but had married into the Quarterhorse family. She was a very talented onstage dancer. Her brother was a well-known actor and comic stage performer who performed in many hit movie musicals and comedies. In fact, that whole side of Joey's family was into theater work of some sort. And it was where he got a large measure of artistic talent and acting ability.

When Joey took to the stage in an acting class, the little colt turned into a graceful stallion and was amazing to watch. Ty had seen a play in which Joey had the lead part, so why the young stud hadn't caught Ty's eye before made him rethink everything. Perhaps he was just hung up on the brawny good looks and muscular bulges of the athletes' bodies. There was nothing more masculine than a well-built Clydesdale. No doubt about it. But now Ty found something very attractive about Joey. There was something adorably cute in this little colt of a stud.

Growing up, Ty often thought what it would be like to be an adult, to be on his own. And as puberty hit, what it would be like to be in love and to have someone love him. So very often now, such thoughts seemed to result in him developing a crush on a fellow stud only to realize that any affections he might show that other stud would result in rejection, maybe even hostility. He quickly learned how to hide his feelings. He could even get away with studying his crush without being detected.

Now things were different. Coming out to his best friend, Kyle, helped set the stage for meeting someone who might actually be interested in him. And it surprised him to find that he already knew Joey but had never given him a second thought. Yet there he was, having romantic thoughts about one of his classmates. One who was open to his affections. And Tyler was a very physically affectionate stud.

Thoughts of Joey began to swirl around in Tyler's mind, crowding out all other thoughts. How Joey looked on stage took over his mind and spread throughout his body. The little colt's graceful moves, the way his rippling muscles showed through his skintight stretch leotards, and how he looked with his loose shirt open down to his belt buckle. Ty's raging hormones had kicked in and were racing at a full gallop.

Once Ty tended to his physical needs, he could get some much-needed rest. Pulling the covers over himself, he drifted off to sleep with wonderful thoughts playing in his mind. Thoughts of Joey. Would that they would all come true. He was in love and with a colt of a stud no less!

CHAPTER 10

Confronted

The next morning Ty awoke feeling fantastic. After last night's session, he finally felt normal and complete, like life was finally worth living. He had no idea how things were about to change for him. Or what lay ahead for him and Joey.

His first thought as he sat up in bed was that he had to find out what Joey thought of him. Was he even attracted by Ty's stallion persona? After all, Ty was one of the best athletes in school and a well-liked stud horse among his mare classmates. He decided to ask Joey at the first opportunity.

His mind obviously on romance, Ty forgot he had gym class first period, and his brown tail was already past the bottom of his butt. He hadn't given it a thought until he got to school, and the realization hit him like a bolt of lightning as he caught his first glimpse of the front doors.

Kyle was walking beside him when Ty stopped dead in his tracks, a look of horror written all over his face. Kyle suddenly realized his friend's condition, and the dilemma.

"What am I going to do?" Ty asked.

"We'll have to think of something to get you out of showering. Maybe if you quietly disappear at some point at the end of class, nobody will notice. I'll do my best to cover for you."

Unfortunately, that plan wasn't going to work as KC was there to make sure. It was he who kept an eye on Tyler, making sure he didn't slip away at the end of class. KC confronted Ty at the door of the locker room. "I'm gonna make sure you shower, Ty," KC said in an almost threatening tone.

Ty knew he was had. KC stood there, watching him strip. Ty paused as he prepared to pull off his gym pants. For an instant, he stood there, back to the locker, and looked around the locker room for any kind of support or friendly face.

Kyle had enough of KC's bullying of Tyler. "So you like watching studs strip, do you, KC?" Kyle called out loudly. "Maybe you're dipping your tail in white paint."

"Now wait a minute, Kyle. I don't do that! But I think Ty's hiding something."

"What business is it of yours, Mr. Studly DoRight?" Kyle snapped back.

"Hey, leave Ty alone," piped in Andy Thoroughbred. "I for one don't care if Ty's tail is brown or white. He's a good friend, and that's his own business, not mine. Or yours."

By then, a crowd had gathered around the studs. But to Ty's surprise, several others started saying the same thing.

Seeing he was outnumbered, KC had no choice but to back down. But as he slowly pulled away, he muttered, "You haven't heard the last of this yet."

Ty could only stand there, surrounded by the friendly faces of the other studs. His support team had suddenly grown. Several of them spoke to him in a positive manner. He could now get dressed without having to expose his tail. This time. Thankfully, he would not have to see KC for the rest of the day.

His next class was language, which he shared with Joey. By the time he got to class, Joey was already seated in the back, a place he normally would never have taken. As soon as their eyes met, he motioned Ty to sit in the next seat over. Ty needed no further invitation and slid in beside Joey.

For once, Tyler actually enjoyed language class. But that might have been because Joey was beside him, and they constantly shared affectionate glances. As the class ended, Ty decided to ask Joey how he felt about him. "Joey," he whispered, "do you feel the same way about me as I do about you?"

"And how would that be?"

They looked at each other. Their eyes met, and Ty could almost feel his heart jump out of his chest. The sparks between them were beginning to ignite in their gaze. "I think you know," was all Ty could whisper.

"I think I do. I mean, I think I'm attracted to you in a major way, Ty."

By now the classroom was empty, except for the teacher. His voice broke their stare. "You two lovebirds better get on to your next class," was all he said. The studs looked at him and then at one another. "Surprised? I couldn't help but see what was going on between you two all during class. That's sweet, so I couldn't bring myself to call on either of you or disturb the mood. But next time, try to pay attention to class."

Ty and Joey now knew that they had another adult's support. They wouldn't share another class together that day, but they sat together at lunch, surrounded like a fortress by an ever-growing group of friends.

It sseemed Kyle, Andy, and Jennifer had been talking to other friends, finding out who was open-minded, who agreed with the latest scientific findings, and just who was religious. They invited the friendly ones to join a new group in support of science and truth over religious dogma.

CHAPTER 11

The New Group

"So what are we going to call our group?" someone asked over the lunch table.

"Don't student groups need a teacher to sponsor them? Who are we going to get?" asked another.

"No problem with that, I think," answered Tyler. "For sure our language teacher will sign on. He caught on to Joey and me during his class."

"Looks like you two are becoming an item," Kyle remarked, which brought an, "Awwww," from the entire group.

"Maybe the science teacher will be interested in sponsoring our group as well," suggested another.

"How could he not?" Andy remarked. "He keeps up with the latest scientific happenings. And we all know what they've been saying lately."

"Yeah, I think religion is due for a reality check." The comments were now flying from everywhere.

"Oh, the theocracy ain't gonna like that!"

"So isn't it about time?" Joey piped in. "Religion has been the basis for a lot of abuse over the centuries, and it's about time it all ends. After all, we're all the same. What's the problem with a little thing like tail color revealing who we really love?"

"Words well spoken, Joey. I knew you kept up on current

events," was heard from the back. Everyone turned around to see their science teacher.

"He is rather outspoken in civics class," someone quipped.

"I'm wondering if science will ever be able to get the religious fanatics to accept their proof," another wondered.

"Well, back a few centuries ago they did finally have to cave in on their old flat Equus idea," the teacher remarked.

"True. But not until after several centuries of denial," someone reminded the group.

"Yes, but that happened long before the internet. Nowadays, everything is on there, and it's impossible to keep anything from becoming known worldwide," remarked another.

"But we'll still have the old-school thinkers, those who will never give up what they were taught as a kid. Even if the truth bashes them in the muzzle," Kyle added.

"I'm afraid my folks are that way," Ty said, looking down at the floor, his eyes starting to tear up. Everyone's attention turned to him.

"You OK, Ty?" Kyle asked, putting his hand on Ty's shoulder.

"I guess I might as well let everybody know," he said. He tearfully looked up at the group. "My parents found out about me and threw me out of the house. Had it not been for Kyle, I'd still be out on the street." He started to cry, and Joey and Kyle immediately threw their arms around him. Others in the group joined in until he overcame the painful thoughts of that day.

Tyler now knew he had a support group to protect him. And the group had solidified behind their desire to change the world around them, even if they only managed to affect their school. The science teacher was behind them as well, and before long, their group seemed to grow considerably as word quietly spread from friend to friend.

That week, the group even spread to the studs in the gym class as they rallied around Ty. They even showered together, allowing Ty to let his growing brown tail show. The other studs in the group never let the difference bother them, which made Ty comfortable with himself. And even more surprising was that the coach never seemed to notice that anything was going on.

Within the first few weeks of school, the language teacher talked privately to Tyler and let him know he supported a formal student group. With two teachers on board and a growing group of supportive friends, what could stop them?

CHAPTER 12

The Proposal

It would be the following week before Tyler had another gym class and would have to worry about another confrontation with KC. Before that was the weekend, and Ty wanted to ask Joey on their first date. The prospect of being alone with another stud, just him and Joey, excited Ty. What would happen? What could happen? He didn't know, but he wanted to find out. He had to ask the little colt at just the right moment.

Even though he saw Joey every day that week in language class, Ty chose to drop by his after-school theater group rehearsal. Maybe there he could find the right moment to ask Joey out. Maybe he could also see him perform on the stage. It was something that seemed to bring out the stallion in the little guy. And that stoked the fire in Ty's furnace.

Sure enough, when he got to the rehearsal hall, Joey was up on stage, rehearsing a scene from their latest assignment. As Joey performed, Ty slipped into a seat at the rear of the theater and watched him. How Joey handled himself onstage was magical in Ty's eyes. No longer the little colt, Joey seemed to become a mighty stallion as he romped around the stage, saying his lines with authority and moving so gracefully. The more he watched, the more attractive he became to Tyler.

Too soon, though, the scene ended, and the cast took a break. Joey looked out into the mostly empty seats. Spotting Ty, he came down off the stage and up the aisle to where Ty sat. Plopping down in the seat next to him, Joey threw an arm around his shoulders.

His free hand reached over and gently moved Ty's muzzle close to his own. Their lips met, and Joey gave Ty a passionate kiss for what seemed like eternity. Too surprised to pull away, Ty could only respond in kind as the fireworks exploded in his mind.

But then he suddenly remembered where he was. He was in public, kissing another stud in front of all the world! Breaking off the kiss, he pulled away just enough to look Joey straight in the eyes. Then they both looked around to see if anyone had seen them.

There on stage were several of the cast, and just as suddenly, they erupted in applause and cheers of "Bravo!" Ty was wide-eyed with surprise.

"It's OK, Ty. They all know about us. It's all over school—but only among the right people."

"You mean, they know about both of us being brown-tails, and they're OK with it?"

"Ok? Heck, they think we make a cute couple!"

"Hey, Joey, bring your sweetheart up here to meet the rest of the cast," one of them shouted.

"Come on. Follow me." Joey stood up and took Ty's hand as he rose from his seat. Ty followed him to the stage.

"Well, when are you two going out on a date?" one of the mares asked. Ty began to blush.

"Well?" another one asked.

What could Ty do but turn to Joey and ask. "Joey, you want to go see a movie with me tonight?"

Throwing his arms around Ty's neck, Joey immediately accepted with a kiss, which received a resounding, "Awwww," from the rest of the cast. But all Ty could see was Joey's face. "Pick me up for dinner at six?" he whispered in Joey's ear. Joey nodded as a smile lit up his face.

CHAPTER 13

The Grooming Session

Tyler wanted to look good for his first date with Joey. He talked Kyle into helping him groom his tail. A teenager would usually ask his father to assist him with the task, but it was just too personal for Ty to ask Mr. Whitehorse to help him out. After all, young stud horses were known to go into heat with a good tail grooming. But Ty felt he would be safe with a straight stud like Kyle doing the task.

By now, Ty's tail had grown out to about midthigh length and was beginning to need regular grooming. But it was still too short for Ty to easily access.

To start with, Kyle had to work out the tangles. "You never had a tail grooming before now?"

"Nope. At first, I trimmed it off. Then when I was living on my own, I never managed to do anything about it, living the way I had to."

"Must have been a hard life, Ty."

"You have no idea, Kyle."

"I'm so sorry for what you went through. But you're safe now. My folks always liked you, and we've always been the best of friends. And we always will be."

"I'm grateful for that, Kyle."

"OK, your tail's all groomed now. I even put on a tail band so that your tail will stay nice and groomed. And it'll be easier for you to manage it."

"Oh, wow! My first tail band," was all Ty could say, admiring his tail.

"Tail bands are the greatest thing since rolled oats. I don't know how the primitive cave horse ever got along without them," Kyle quipped.

"Think maybe Joey might be the one?" Ty asked.

"The way you two look at each other? Heck, even I can see the sparks flying between you two. Just don't rush things though. After all, this is your first date with him. What are friends for if you can't help them out once in a while?"

"You're the best friend a stud could have, Kyle."

Just then the doorbell rang. "Hope that's not Joey. I'm not dressed yet."

"Well, now would be a good time to wear your tail briefs and jeans. At least until you two go out to the movies. Then you can tuck your tail in."

"Good thing your parents are out for the evening, and you and your sister have dates."

"I'll go answer the door. You get dressed."

As Kyle headed for the front door, Ty got up and slid into his new tail briefs. As he adjusted their fit, he looked at his image in the mirror. *What a hot stud I am,* he thought. Slipping into his tail jeans, he carefully pulled his freshly groomed tail through the break in the rear seam and pulled the jeans up. The elastic tail band sure helped, he discovered. What a stallion he was! And with a handsome, well-groomed brown tail in back, Ty was ready for his evening with his sweetheart stud horse.

"Ty, your stud's here," Kyle yelled from the living room. Ty left the bedroom and headed down the hall. "My folks and sister are gone already, and I'm leaving for my date as well. You two will have the place to yourselves. At least until about midnight, anyway. Don't do anything I wouldn't do." Kyle said with a wink as he went out the front door.

There was Joey, standing there before Ty. Their eyes met, and Ty felt the sparks fly between them. "Hi," was all he could manage to squeak out past the lump in his throat.

"You look handsome tonight," Joey said softly. "And I love your tail jeans. Really brings out the stallion in you."

"And you look ... fantastic, Joey."

"Well, let me slip my tail out. Then tell me what you think." Joey reached around back and carefully pulled his brown, full-length, adult tail out of the seam split in his jeans. "There, now I feel better."

"You look better too. You're a real stallion yourself."

The two wrapped their arms wrapped around each other and were muzzle to muzzle. Slowly their mouths drew closer. When their lips met, Ty could feel the passion in Joey's kiss. Ty kissed back with equal passion, and the sparks flew. Their kiss seemed to last forever, but not long enough, as they slowly parted.

"I've been thinking about you ever since this afternoon at the rehearsal," Ty whispered.

"Me too. After you left, just about everyone in the cast came up to me and congratulated me on finding such a handsome stud friend. The mares were all giddy about how muscular you are. Even some of the other stud horses said they were almost jealous of you, being such an athlete and all."

"And how do you feel?"

"Like I'm the luckiest stud horse on the planet!"

"No, *I* am the luckiest stud horse on the planet, Joey. I have you in my arms."

All Joey could say was, "Awwwww."

The two snuggled, nuzzling each other and gently stroking the other's body. But then they realized that they had to get going, or they might not have enough time for a bite to eat before the movie. Pulling apart, they helped each other tuck in their tails before heading out the door. Joey had a car, so he drove. But he asked Ty where he wanted to eat. Ty picked the Old Feedbag Café, a popular hangout for many in their new support group as well as the drama/theater class.

CHAPTER 14

The First Date

The Old Feedbag Café had been a popular teen date destination for years, with just the right number of open-space tables and more private booths set in cozy stall spaces along the outer walls. Even the old barn exterior presented a warm, inviting image for the high school crowd to gather. By the time Ty and Joey entered, it seemed like all their friends were already there. Andy Thoroughbred and his mare friend, Jennifer Trotter, were beside each other in a booth, with another couple on the other side. Both couples were nuzzling between sips of their drinks.

Kyle stood with his date next to him, a young filly Ty knew only passingly from school. As Ty and Joey entered, a number of friends greeted them or waved. Kyle spotted them and waved them over.

"Hi! Glad you two made it," Kyle said. "This is Amanda."

"I've seen you two around school," Amanda said softly. "I heard some of the other studs talking about you. Sorry to say, some of it wasn't nice."

"I kinda figured there'd be gossip generated about us," Joey admitted.

"They made me pretty uncomfortable and irritated," Amanda stated. "And you know it was KC leading them on."

"Figures," Kyle said. "But at least here you're among friends."

"Yeah. Joey and I just want to enjoy the evening together," Ty said. "And it looks like a nice crowd tonight. Let's find an open booth."

"Sounds good to me. Wanna split a pizza?" Amanda asked.

The two couples spotted a booth opening up right in the middle of the room and slid in. Pizza and drinks were ordered, and various friends came past to greet them.

"It's OK with us if you want to be romantic in front of us," Amanda said. Kyle smiled and nodded. "After all, I know *we* aren't going to hold back." Kyle took Amanda's hand and softly nuzzled her. She responded by planting a big kiss on his mouth.

Ty couldn't hold back any longer. Taking their lead, he planted a kiss on Joey. Before long, both couples were snuggled in each other's arms, nuzzling one another. But the food and drinks came and broke up the intensely romantic mood. And the server didn't bat an eye over the two studs snuggled together.

"Incoming!" she announced, setting the pizza down and serving the drinks. "I heard about you two at school. You *do* make a cute couple," she remarked with a wink. Ty blushed.

"Yes, word is spreading around. I'm just glad you two got together," Kyle responded, looking at Ty and Joey. "You're too nice a stud not to have someone in your life, Ty. After all, I wouldn't be your friend if you weren't such a good person. And I've always thought that Joey was a nice classmate. You two hang on to each other, you hear? I'm rooting for you both."

"Tell you the truth, Joey," Amanda added, "I've been aware of your talent in drama class, and I thought you'd make a good husband for some lucky stud." Joey's jaw dropped. "I kind of figured you might be a brown-tail, but I'm OK with that. You've always been a sensitive and caring stud, and we mares pick up on that. So don't look so surprised."

Joey was now blushing as well. "Guess it's a little harder to hide than I thought," he returned.

"All I know is that when Ty told me, I was a little surprised," Kyle added. "But then he told me what he went through over the summer, and that really tore me up."

"Well, here's to better days," Ty said, picking up his glass. They all joined in with the toast. Then over slices of pizza, the conversation turned to what movies they liked. Joey and Amanda liked romances, while Ty and Kyle, being athletes, favored action movies. But for a date, they all agreed on romantic comedies, but just different ones. So they decided to take in different movies.

When it was time to leave, each couple went to different theaters. Tyler and Joey went to a new romantic comedy. They caught the first evening's showing, which let out early, allowing them to arrive home well before midnight. It also put them in a romantic mood.

Alone together at home, they again pulled their tails out of their jeans. Feeling his oats, Ty could be openly affectionate to Joey. After turning on some romantic music, he reached out to Joey, and the little colt willingly snuggled into Ty's muscular arms. The couple slow danced to the music, gently moving about and nuzzling each other. After a while, they sat on the couch to snuggle.

"You having as good a time as I am?" Ty whispered in Joey's ear.

"Yes, I think so," he responded. "I sure enjoyed the movie. It was even better being with you."

"I'm glad we were able to sit in back without anyone around. I could hold your hand through most of the movie."

"That was my most favorite part" Joey said. "It's actually the first time I've ever held another stud's hand. You have such perfect hands. And the rest of you isn't bad either."

"I hoped that you'd see me as more than just a well-built stud."

"Oh, I do. I'm not just saying you have a great body. You do, but you're so kind and gentle too. But I'm most attracted to what's inside you. You're more than just a well-built athlete. I'm just not sure what you see in me."

"Well, some may see you as just a little colt. But when you're onstage, you're absolutely amazing. I don't think I've ever seen any stud look so masculine."

"Love you," Joey whispered in Ty's ear.

"Love you too," Ty whispered in return.

By the time Kyle's family began arriving home, the two lovebirds were asleep in bed, snuggled together, arm in arm, behind the closed door of Ty's bedroom.

CHAPTER 15

Resistance

Pastor Joe Clydesdale had not only preached hellfire against brown-tail studs and stallions, he was also the chief elder on the Council of Elders, which governed the world. Marie Clydesdale led scripture classes at church that emphasized condemnation of brown-tails. Even KC's older brother, Chris, had been involved in gang beatings of brown-tail studs and stallion couples. He had even beaten one young brown-tail stud so badly that the kid spent several weeks in the hospital. He survived but was crippled for life. His supportive parents tried to have Chris arrested, but all the religious police did was warm him verbally not to kill anyone in the future. Even their lawsuit against Chris was thrown out of court.

The Clydesdale family was so influential it could generate lots of public opinion against any student group that supported a white-tail/brown-tail coalition. That was a paradigm shift KC's parents would not tolerate. Marie was also on the school board, so when news of the new group reached their ears, it threw more gasoline on the fire. There was no way she was going to allow such a thing, even with two teachers' sponsorship. And if she had her way, those teachers might also be forced to resign. All of which would make for a very fiery school board meeting.

The worship day before that meeting, Pastor Joe made sure the subject of his sermon was the problem of brown-tails and their corruption of society. With that sermon, he managed to whip the congregation into a frenzy of fear and hatred. As would be their custom, Tyler's parents were active members of the congregation and in attendance that morning. When they heard Pastor Joe announce their son's name, they were horrified. Ty's mother was embarrassed to tears.

While Mrs. Palomino cried, Mr. Palomino angerly denounced Ty and his group of friends. "He's no son of mine anymore," he declared. "I threw him out of the house the day we found out because he refused to repent from his evil ways. He's an embarrassment to me, and I won't be held responsible for his rebelliousness! Lord knows, his mother and I did everything we could to raise him right. Where we failed, we don't know. Now he's infected a whole gang of sinners and turned the school into a den of iniquity. We're ashamed and disheartened."

After the impromptu speech, family friends gathered around the Palominos, comforting Mrs. Palomino and offering them their backing with hugs and words of support. But Pastor Joe wasn't finished. "The school board is meeting tomorrow evening, and I ask that as many of this congregation be there to support our efforts to eliminate this new threat to our religion and way of life. And I'll be there to back up Marie's efforts." He knew she had plans of her own. She not only wanted to expel the offending students, she planned to demand that the sponsoring teachers be forced to resign.

Meanwhile, KC and Chris had plans of their own, unbeknown to their parents. Chris had graduated the year before and had joined a fraternity house at college. So while KC rounded up his high school buddies on the sports teams, Chris was going to get a group of his frat brothers to join them in an effort to inflict some bodily harm on the insurrection leaders. At the top of their list were Ty and Joey as having an openly brown-tail couple in school didn't sit well with him.

The two planned to have their combined gangs corner the couple on their way to school and do something to them rather than turning them in to the Morality Police. Certainly the college studs had the strength to subdue the two colt-friends and any of their support group who may be protecting them. KC had been shadowing the two ever since they got together and had picked out the spot. And after their religion's apparent stamp of approval, the stage was set. Now all the brothers' gang had to do to spring their trap was lie in wait the next morning.

CHAPTER 16

The Assault

On their way to school, Joey and Ty would drive through one of the city parks. It was usually an unoccupied stretch of secluded parkland. But that morning, it was where KC, Chris, and their gang set up their blockade for their ambush. Sure enough, as regular as clockwork, the couple drove right into the trap at the expected time.

Joey and Ty were enjoying the peaceful morning's commute to school when they were suddenly stopped by two cars blocking the road. They recognized KC, so Joey quickly threw the car in reverse. But before he could turn around, another car came from behind to block the couple in. It was Chris and a car full of college studs. At that moment, all the Clydesdales's gang members jumped out of the cars and dragged the two out of Joey's car.

Tyler was strong enough to resist for a while. He put up a brave fight, but against four or five college athletes, he was no match. Meanwhile, Joey was quickly subdued. Before Ty realized it, someone had put a noose around Joey's neck, and the little colt was dragged under a large tree. As Tyler was wrestled to the ground, he managed to look up to see Joey being reeled by the neck up and on to one of the tree's large branches.

"Joey!" cried out Ty. But the little colt could only flail about, a look of horror on his face. With the rope tied securely, Joey hung in midair. Ty could only watch him struggle as the gang had securely bound Ty and tied him to a smaller tree with a clear view of Joey.

Then they all left the area, leaving Ty to watch helplessly while Joey strangled, hanging from the tree limb. "Joey, I love you! Joey!" cried Ty. "Somebody help us," Ty screamed as loudly as he could. But there was no one around to hear him. "Joey, my little Joey," Ty managed to get out before the tears choked his cries. He was bawling like a baby as he managed to get out one more scream, "Help!" Then all he could do was watch Joey's body go still and lifeless.

Just then, a car came down the park road, suddenly accelerating to the scene and coming to a screeching halt. Out jumped Kyle, Andy, and two more friends. They all raced to Joey. A couple of them grabbed hold of his limp body as the others scrambled to untie the rope. Releasing it, Joey collapsed into the studs' arms. They quickly laid him on the ground and began CPR; fortunately, two had been trained in it just the week before. Meanwhile, Jennifer was in the car, frantically dialing for help.

Kyle and the other stud then ran over to Tyler and began to free him. "Joey," was all Ty could manage to say. "My little Joey ..."

"Ty, we'll do what we can," Kyle said. "How long has he been there?"

"Too long, too long," Kyle sobbed through his tears.

"Who did this?" Andy asked.

"It was KC, his brother Chris, and a bunch of guys I didn't recognize."

"Must have been some of Chris's college buddies, I bet." Kyle said as the last of Ty's bindings were undone. Ty immediately leaped up and raced to Joey's side as the two studs furiously kept working on him.

Just then, the emergency squad came screaming up, followed by a police car. The EMTs jumped out of the ambulance and rushed over to them, equipment in hand. They quickly took over from the studs, who were exhausted by now. All Ty and the others could do was stand by and watch. And hope. Ty collapsed, sobbing, into Kyle's and Jennifer's arms.

After the EMTs loaded Joey into the ambulance, they asked one of the police officers to take Tyler to the hospital for them; they couldn't take both in the ambulance. They wanted to check Ty out and make sure he wasn't hurt, but they were too occupied to do that at the park. As the ambulance raced away, Ty and Kyle climbed into the police car. They followed the ambulance's path to the hospital. One officer questioned Ty as the other drove.

Ty was guarded about revealing his relationship with Joey, but it was too obvious to the officers. So the one driving volunteered a little bit of personal information. "Son, if it will help, let me tell you something about my family. My partner knows and is fine with it. You see, my nephew is a brown-tail, and was arrested by the Morality Police. So I know what they do to minors in those camps, and I am personally appalled. But being a law officer myself, I am in a difficult position, so I choose to look the other way. It's not easy, but I can live with myself a lot easier. So until things change, all I can do is tell you that I am sympathetic to you and your colt-friend."

Ty broke down and opened up. Both officers promised they would write it up in a way that would keep the Morality Police off the case.

When they arrived at the hospital, Ty leaped out of the cruiser and bolted into the ER, demanding to see Joey. It took both the police officers and the hospital security guard to restrain him until he calmed down. The medical staff checked him out and gave him an all clear.

"Let me see Joey," Ty demanded. The hospital staff refused as he wasn't family, so he didn't have any rights. The police officers and hospital security guard again had to restrain him.

Ty unexpectedly slugged the guard, knocking him out with a single blow, and bolted out of the room. He ran down the hall, looking in every room he came across. Finally, he found Joey in an ICU room and attempted to rush to his side. But by now, hospital security had caught up with him. It took several guards to restrain him and drag him into the hall.

"I want to see Joey," Ty demanded.

"That why you slugged me?" a guard asked.

"Sorry I did that. All I want is to see him. He needs me, and I need him."

"What's the story here?" a voice came from down the hall. A distinguished-looking stallion appeared from among the commotion swirling around Tyler. He quickly identified himself as a university scientist, and he had been listening on his scanner as the story unfolded.

One of the security guard officers turned and filled him in on what happened. But none of the hospital staff would give any details to him or Ty as to Joey's condition.

"Tyler, I was able to convince the officer not to press charges. I recognized him through my research studies, and I know his only son is a brown-tail. So he's sympathetic to you. He was just doing his job, so go easy on him, OK? That said, tell me what happened this morning and your connection to Joey. And son," said the scientist quietly, "I know you're a brown-tail, so you don't have to hide anything. He's your colt friend, isn't he?"

51

"Yes," Ty said, tears rolling down his cheeks. "I love him, and he loves me. I don't want to lose him." He sobbed.

"Ty, I know you do. But I have news that will really help you and all brown-tails. Let me get the doctor in here. Maybe my news will move the doc to allow you to see Joey."

He called the doc into the room and shared his news, which left everyone wide-eyed and stunned. The scientist then told them about the school board meeting called for that evening. "I'm sorry, but I have to go and prepare for the evening."

After the scientist left, the doctor agreed to let Tyler see Joey. He escorted him past the rest of the staff and to Joey's side. The doc had advised Ty that Joey was in a coma. "We don't know when or if he will come out of it," said the doctor.

Ty took Joey's hand and held it tight as he leaned over and whispered in Joey's ear, "I love you. Please don't leave me. I can't live without you." Ty then softly kissed Joey's muzzle.

CHAPTER 17

꙰

All Hell Breaks Loose

The school board meeting room was packed to overflowing. Pastor Joe was in the front row of the public seating area, while Marie sat behind a long table with the rest of the school board members. The board chair-horse almost had to yell in order to quiet the crowd and start the meeting.

"Attention, mares and stallions! This meeting shall come to order," he said. "The first item on our agenda is this matter of the formation of a white-tail/brown-tail student group." A big commotion erupted from the crowd.

"This is heresy," cried Pastor Joe. Many in the crowd began shouting similar comments.

"Quiet down!" yelled the chair-horse. "You'll all get to have your say at the right time."

More shouting from the crowd ensued. "Quiet, or I'll adjourn the meeting here and now!" The crowd finally calmed down, though murmuring persisted.

"May I address the meeting?" Marie asked, raising her hand.

"Granted," said the chair-horse.

"My friends, we all know what the scripture says about brown-tails. We cannot allow them to pollute our children's minds. This was all the doing of just two students who are now flaunting their brown tails in public. I am appalled!" More shouts came from the crowd, which the chair-horse quickly silenced. Marie continued,

"We must keep our schools free from the evil and immoral deeds of these two sinners. I move that they be expelled, and the two teachers who foolishly chose to try to sponsor this horrible idea be asked, no, be forced to resign for the good of our precious children."

Pastor Joe yelled, "Amen," with many of the crowd joining in several rounds more of "Amen. Amen."

"Quiet, everyone," shouted the chair-horse again. The crowd grew even more restless.

"I object!" came a voice from back. It was the science teacher. "Let him speak," came from someone on the other side of the room.

"Marie, are you finished?" asked the chair-horse.

She responded with a simple, "Yes."

"Thank you, Mrs. Clydesdale. And Mr. Chair-horse," the teacher continued, "I have just come from the hospital, where one of these two students, admittedly brown-tails, were taken after both were attacked by a gang of thugs while on their way to school this morning. Seems that one student was lynched." Gasps arose from the crowd. "He was left hanging from a tree. The other student was tied to another tree. He could only watch helplessly while his stud-friend was hung right in front of him and left to strangle." More gasps arose from the crowd.

The gasps were understandable. In the history of the planet, no murders had ever taken place. Horse-people had always been peaceful and nonviolent. So even the idea of such a crime was so shocking to the audience that everyone sat there in total horror, their lower jaws on the floor, and their eyes as big as the bottom of a feedbag.

"However, by a fortunate stroke of luck, some other students' timely arrival on the scene broke up the lynching. They also called the emergency squad, and he was taken to the hospital, where he is in ICU as we speak. As yet, we don't know whether their quick action and CPR training have saved this young stud's life. We're awaiting word as to whether he will even survive, let alone if he'll have any lasting injuries. The last I heard, if he does make it, he may have some brain damage." More gasps came from the crowd.

The university scientist then stood and spoke. "Friends, as dire as this news is, I have come to this meeting to let everyone know that there is nothing to fear from brown-tails. "In fact, I have been part of the scientific community closely concerning brown-tails, and would like to be one of the first to let you all know of a breakthrough scientific discovery that is just now being broadcast all over the world by way of the internet. Scientists have been working on the origins of the brown-tail occurrences, and have made a significant discovery. They have discovered that in predictably one in twenty times, when the DNA strands from an egg and a sperm join, there occurs something remarkable. A new gene is spontaneously created, one that scientists have been able to determine is in every brown-tail, but is never found in white-tails. And even more remarkable is that this happens every one in twenty times with male children, without anything influencing it. In simple words, brown-tails are totally natural for one in every twenty child who is born, and there is nothing we can do about it! Brown-tails are a totally natural variation and *not* a choice. It is similar to the spontaneous generation of being left side oriented. Ultimately, religion must bow to science when science proves something to be true. This is such a case. Our religion has taught for generations that brown-tails are unnatural and a conscious decision on the part of the individual who wants to sin against the Great One. Well, this scientific breakthrough has disproven that. So now our theocracy is going to have to change their laws to reflect this, or our religion will face being laughed into obscurity. The ball is now in the government's court. And Pastor Joe, since you are on the Council of Elders, you must change your views and do something positive."

The room fell into total silence. Pastor Joe and Marie sat there, wide-eyed and in shock.

Silence was finally broken when the chair-horse was the first to speak. "Mrs. Clydesdale's motion is declared invalid," he announced. "And this meeting is adjourned." With that, what was once an overflow crowd quietly began to dissipate.

CHAPTER 18

Day of Reckoning

The morning after the school board meeting, the Council of Elders was called into a secret emergency session. News of this new scientific discovery would be devastating to the very foundations of the theocratic government, even to their religion. Damage control was utmost on their minds. Technology not only enabled such news to be spread quickly worldwide but allowed the council's sessions to be carried out by way of video conferencing. The Council of Elders had to take control of the situation and figure out how to diffuse it lest they and their religion be destroyed altogether.

It was like the old flat Equus belief of half a millennium ago. Until then, religious leaders had insisted that the world was flat because the sacred scriptures implied that. But the scientists persisted, and along with explorations of the world by early adventurers looking for unclaimed worldly valuables, it was proven that the world was round. When that fact became common knowledge, the Council of Elders had been forced into renouncing the flat-world teachings and take an abstract interpretation of what they previously said was their religious truth.

The religion-based government barely survived that revelation. But a quick reinterpretation of the scriptures saved their theocracy. And that is what they needed now. According to tradition, the oldest of the elders took charge of the board meeting. Elder Joe could not be located, so that duty fell to Elder Bill, who opened the meeting with a call to order and roll call. Once everyone else had checked in, he summarized the situation to the rest of the group.

"Elders, this situation is going to become critical within the next few hours, and we have to come up with a solution. With the latest scientific news, it's apparent that we need a new interpretation of the scriptures. And more so, a good cover-up for the past interpretation and our actions accordingly. Anyone have any suggestions?"

"Can't we just denounce the kid as a heretic, like we have all those busybody scientists who claimed we evolved from lesser animals?" one of them asked.

"No, that's not going to work this time. Nobody has ever had an out-of-body experience and said anything about meeting the Great One. Nor has anyone been nearly murdered and come back with any stories. It's the kid's hanging that makes this story believable. We've got to sound even more believable," Elder Bill stated. "Any other suggestions?'

None of the elders could come up with anything plausible, except for Elder John. "As I see the scriptures, they're all about loving one another. We horse-people have always been a peaceful species, and as such, I think we can use those parts of the scripture that back up this viewpoint and say that the few verses we've been using to condemn brown-tails were misinterpreted all along. After all, none of the direct words of the Great One ever say that brown-tails are or should be looked down on, let alone despised. Maybe we can smooth over the whole incident by claiming that we overlooked the Great One's intent, that it's those few verses that we misinterpreted, and admit that we have misinterpreted the Great One's directive."

"Sounds like you have a good handle on that viewpoint, Elder John," said Elder Bill. "I'm appointing you to lead a committee of your choice to write a proper statement explaining this new view, along with something that will explain how we ever misinterpreted the scriptures, and how our misinterpretation can be seen as understandable under the circumstances. We also need Elder Ralph to contact everyone on the internet as to this news. Elder Ralph?"

There was a pause, and then Elder Ralph responded, "Elders, I have been monitoring the internet as we have been talking, and there is yet more news. And this one is really bad." He began to choke up. As tears started to stream down his cheeks, he managed to cough up the words, "They've found Elder Joe."

CHAPTER 19

Center of the Storm

That same morning, the news-horses had surrounded Pastor Joe's home. It was all the police could do to hold them back so the EMTs could go about their business.

Earlier that night, Pastor Joe and Marie came home in silence after the disastrous meeting. All Joe could do was sit in his easy chair while Marie went to the kitchen to pour herself a glass of her special "cooking sherry." She then came into the room and sat down on the couch beside Joe's chair.

The silence was broken when a door down the hall creaked open. KC and Chris slowly stepped into the room. Chris spoke for them both. "Mom, Dad, we've done something horrible, along with several of my frat brothers."

"We know, son," Joe said in low voice. He looked up into the studs' faces. "But why?" For the first time that KC could remember, he saw tears running down his father's cheeks.

"Dad," he finally spoke, "things just got out of hand. I don't know what got into Chris's frat buddies, but going into it, I thought we were just going to tie the two brown-tails up and humiliate them. I didn't expect they were going to lynch the little stud and leave him hanging. It was meant only to be a joke, to scare the little stud and his stud-friend." By now both Chris and KC were crying.

Suddenly, there came a loud knock on the door. Marie shook

off her surprise and quickly went to answer the door. The next thing they knew, the room was filled with police officers.

Officer Dave spoke first. "Are you two Chris and Kurt Clydesdale?" The studs nodded. "You are under arrest for attempted murder. Come with us." The studs were strapped into harnesses and led away.

Pastor Joe got up out of his easy chair, and without saying a word, retired to his study and closed the door. Marie walked back to the kitchen, grabbed the bottle of sherry, and plopped into a kitchen chair. She couldn't remember how long she sat there, but by morning, the bottle was empty. As the empty glass slipped out of her hand and fell to the floor, the sound of it shattering startled her awake.

She slowly arose from the kitchen chair, her head reeling from a hangover, and managed to stand up. The details of the previous night still played in her mind. *What to do now?* she wondered. She worked her way down the hall to Pastor Joe's study. The door was locked. It was not like her husband to have the door locked. She called out, but there was no response. She banged on the door. Still no reply. Then she remembered the spare key on the transom. She retrieved it, slipped it in the lock, turned the key, and opened the door. As it swung open, what she saw was too much. Marie fainted.

The phone rang again, as the Council of Elders tried to call. Various elders had been calling all night long, but even they would be shocked by what Marie saw. There in the doorway to the private washroom off the study was Pastor Joe's lifeless body, hanging from the door's transom.

By that morning, the police had KC and Chris in custody, along with the rest of those who took part in the crime. But without any leadership from the Board of Elders or anyone else in the government, all they could do was keep them locked up.

All the elders were in hiding. By midday they were holding their second emergency online conference.

"With the loss of Elder Joe Clydesdale, I am going to have to take over permanent charge of our meetings," declared Elder Bill. "Elder John, have you worked up that statement you were asked to compose? Does it take this latest scientific discovery into consideration?"

"I have, with Elder Ralph's help. I feel that with any luck, we may yet salvage the government. We will have to admit that religion must bow to scientific discoveries and that since science deals only what is provable, religion will hereafter deal only with what is not provable. Any interpretations of the scriptures will also have to pass that requirement. I know this is a big leap for us, but we have no choice. This incident has backed us into a corner, and this is our only way out lest we be laughed into obscurity."

"I've prepared a statement to that effect, if it meets with everyone's approval," added Elder Ralph. "It'll go out with just a touch of a button." A vote was then called for, and all the board approved. "Then it will be done."

Just as the Board of Elders' statement was going out, the media's attention was focused on Joey's recovery and eventual statement. What he was going to say would cause the elders' statement to be lost in the wait for any news.

CHAPTER 20

Awakening

At the hospital, the vigil over Joey continued throughout that first night. The staff had put up his parents in an adjacent room, but Ty had refused to leave Joey's side and bravely sat at his bedside holding his hand. By morning, Ty had drifted off to sleep, still holding on to Joey. None of the hospital staff disturbed the two, even though they regularly checked on Joey's condition. It was midmorning before Tyler woke up. Even though he was hungry, he refused to leave his bedside vigil. Finally, he broke down and asked the staff for something to eat. They brought him a bowl of oats. It was the first food he had eaten since the morning before.

Maybe it was the sound of Ty's crunching of oats or his constant talking to Joey between each spoonful, but Joey began to stir. His eyes slowly opened, and as he looked up into Ty's face, a tear trickled down his cheek. He wasn't alone with that as tears were also rolling down Ty's face. Their eyes locked together, and a twinkle came into Joey's eyes. Ty's heart leaped for joy.

As Ty drew closer to Joey, the door swung open, and the doctor appeared. At first the sight of Joey awake momentarily stopped him. His eyes opened wide, and his mouth dropped open. But he quickly recovered his composure. "Well, this is good to see! Joey, can you say something to me?" Joey turned to look at the doc and could only manage a hoarse whisper. Even Ty couldn't make out what he tried to say. "That's OK. Just rest. Let me check your vitals, and then I'll let you two alone. Just as long as you let him rest. OK, Tyler?" Ty nodded. The doc went about his work and then, true to his word, left.

The press had gathered in the hospital lobby that morning. The public had also started to gather, and soon the lobby was filled to overflowing. By midmorning, the crowd had filled the parking lot, and brought traffic to a halt. Joey's doctor then appeared in front of the waiting press and crowd to make the announcement.

"Good morning, everyone," the doctor began. "I know you are all awaiting news of the condition of Joey Quarterhorse, the young stud viciously attacked by a gang of thugs. He was hung from a tree and left to die. Had it not been for a group of high school studs who appeared at just the right time, this young stud might have died. I have good news. I've just come from his bedside, and he has awakened from the coma." Cheers erupted from the crowd, drowning out the doctor's call for calm. Word spread to the crowd outside, and more cheers arose.

Finally, the doctor was able to continue. "As of yet, we don't know if he has suffered any brain damage or its possible extent. When we do know more, we will let you all know. But at least he is out of danger and on the way to recovery." More cheers erupted from the crowd.

The news events of the past evening and the morning after had electrified the world. First was the attempted murder, something that had never happened before in recorded history. Then was the turbulent board meeting, where there was at first expected a religious shutdown of the organization of a white-tail/brown-tail student alliance. Instead, it had been turned upside down by the revelation of new scientific evidence. That evidence sent the religious government into total chaos and caused their legal establishment to go into hiding. The arrest of two sons of one of the most powerful elders on the board only compounded the situation. Then when news broke of the elder's suicide, all hell broke loose.

The public was in total revolt against their religious government, and the elders were losing all control. Calls for a new government based on scientific truths rather than religious texts came from all quarters of the world. Public demonstrations and protest rallies erupted in countless cities, and the elders in all communities were nowhere to be seen. What was needed was some good news, so the crowd around the hospital grew and grew. News crews from nearby towns began setting up relay speaker systems and large video screens along the streets, block by block, leading to the hospital.

The news of Joey's survival and awakening from his coma was greeted with worldwide enthusiasm and calls for support and acceptance of brown-tails. It was an amazing overnight turnaround in the public's attitudes about this previously controversial issue.

After the quick press briefing, the doctor returned to Joey's room and asked Tyler to give him a few minutes to examine his patient. Reluctantly, Ty slowly made his way to the door and stepped outside, never losing sight of Joey until closing the door behind him.

The doctor sat down beside Joey's bed and asked him to talk to him. Joey's throat was still badly bruised from the hanging, so all he could manage was a coarse whisper, "What do you want to talk about, doc?"

"Tell me what you remember before waking up here."

"I remember being dragged out of the car by several stallions. One was KC from school. They simply overpowered us. They dragged me over to a tree and threw a rope around my neck. Next thing I knew, the rope tightened around my neck, and I was hoisted into the air. I couldn't call out for help as I struggled against the rope. My hooves were off the ground, so the rope got really tight. Before long, I couldn't even breathe. Then I seemed to go to sleep." Joey's voice was even more hoarse.

"That's all I needed to know," said the doctor. "You sound like you still have all your mental capacity and memories. Do you remember what your life was like before the attack?"

"I know I love Ty. He's such a nice horse, so kind and gentle. And he's got such a gorgeous physique and is so handsome. Everything I could ever want in a stallion." He could barely whisper by now.

"I think you should rest now. Your throat has been badly bruised, and we need to give it time to heal. So don't say anything more for a while. I'll tell Ty to keep you silent for a while too. You two can communicate with notes. OK?" Joey nodded.

As the doctor opened the door to leave, Tyler came through the door first. The doc cautioned him to give Joey's throat some time to heal, and Ty promised he would. The doctor also told him that he felt there was no brain damage. Ty breathed a sigh of relief. The doctor then left the two alone.

The next morning a nurse came in to take orders for lunch and told Joey that he would be limited to things that would be easy for him to swallow. She suggested a smoothie. Joey reluctantly agreed. Tyler asked if he could have something more filling. The nurse knew exactly what to bring and then left the two alone.

Joey had already been busy writing notes. So many, in fact, that they soon had to request more paper. By lunchtime, Joey had completed what he needed to write. It wasn't just communications with Ty but something much bigger. Ty was amazed. Joey had written all morning and was pretty tired, but he was still hungry enough that he asked for a double portion. The hospital staff was more than happy to oblige him.

The doctor dropped by right after lunch. He was pleased with Joey's progress. But when he saw all Joey had written, he recommended complete rest.

"Not a problem. I'm tired," Joey wrote on his last piece of paper.

"Can I still stay with him?" asked Ty. From the looks on both the studs' faces, how could they be refused?

The doctor updated the waiting press and crowd. The cheers were deafening. While the faces may have shifted from time to time, the sheer size of the crowd didn't waver. By morning, the entire world's theocratic government had lost all control, and it was left up to the local police forces to maintain order. Yet throughout world turmoil, the public's interest in this unlikely romance seemed to stabilize society.

By the next morning, Joey had recovered his voice and could speak normally. The doctor arrived just after breakfast and gave Joey a clean bill of health. But it's what Joey asked him to do that would really shock the world.

"Are you sure you want to tell your story to the public?" the doctor asked.

"I've never been so sure of anything in my life."

"You realize what you could start?" he asked.

"All the more reason to do it," Ty remarked.

CHAPTER 21

The Statement

By the time Joey's throat healed enough for him to speak, he and Tyler had written their way through several reams of paper. At first, the hospital staff wanted to toss the sheets into the trash, but Ty wouldn't let them. And as it turned out, it was a good thing for what Joey had written was what he experienced, starting that fateful morning he and the love of his life were on their way to school to him awakening in the hospital to Tyler's soft voice. The news of his experience had leaked out to the press in teasing bits and pieces, but it was enough to shake society to the core. So the press had formed an encampment around the hospital, forcing the staff to call a press conference and for Joey to speak to them directly.

About midmorning. the doctor appeared in front of a packed room of reporters and the public. A hush fell across the crowd as the doctor approached the microphone.

"Mares and stallions, it is my pleasure to announce that Joey Quarterhorse has recovered enough from his injuries to be able to address the public. What he has to say in his own words is something for which I have no explanation. But I also have no explanation for his remarkably quick recovery. So I now present to you Joey Quarterhorse." Cheers arose with the doctor's last word.

A hush fell over the packed room as Joey was wheeled in, his wheelchair pushed by Tyler. He was flanked by the scientist who created the initial furor at the board meeting. They stopped beside the podium. Joey slowly stood and approached the microphone.

Reading softly from a single sheet, he said, "Mares and stallions, thank you for your interest in what I have experienced recently. I will limit my statement to the revelation I am sure will be of the most interest to everyone. I will post a compete transcript of my experience on the internet in due time. In part, here is what I saw.

"I remember that as I gasped for air and lost consciousness, I found myself in a tunnel of light, traveling at a full gallop toward the brightest light I've ever seen. As I came out of the tunnel, I burst into a wide-open pasture brightly illuminated by something that seemed to come from everywhere. The air was fresh and sweet, and I could take in a deep breath for the first time since that rope had tightened around my neck. Everything seemed to be singing; the sounds were the most beautiful I have ever heard. It was glorious!" A look of seriousness came over Joey as he continued speaking to the stunned audience.

"I saw other horse-people around the pasture. Some I didn't recognize, while there were others that I did. All were stallions and mares who had passed on. Then I saw Jamie Colter waving at me. He was overjoyed to see me and galloped up to me. I was thrilled to see him, and we hugged. He told me he had made a mistake in hanging himself, but that the Great One had intentionally made him a brown-tail. He was supposed to live out his life instead of harming himself. But the Great One still loved him so much that He brought him to heaven so that he could be close to Him and would never feel unloved again. And I could tell that Jamie was much loved. He was so happy!

"What came next is the surprise. I was approached by the most majestic pure-white stallion I have ever seen. He was white from mane to hoof, except for a brown tail." A soft collective gasp arose from the crowd. Joey continued, "He addressed me by name, and I instantly knew exactly who He was. He was the Great One.

"He began by saying 'Joey Quarterhorse, My dear colt, as much as I love you, it is not your time to be here. But I brought you here for a reason. You are much loved and favored by Me, and I need someone to tell My people that enough is enough.' He then told me a lot of important things and instructed me to tell everyone, 'Those who profess to represent Me have My words all wrong. I have chosen you to tell My people that everyone is to be respected and cared for as equally loved horse-people. I made everyone different—some slightly so, some greatly so—because I love diversity. And I made some studs to be attracted to one another. To those I gave a brown tail. Yet some have misinterpreted My words and used them to justify their intolerances.'

"But why did you give us different colored tails?" I asked.

"He answered my question by saying, 'Love is love. I love both genders equally since I made both males and females. So to those who would love someone of the opposite gender, I gave them a white tail. To those who would love someone of their own gender, I gave them a brown tail. I did so in order to allow them to find each other more easily.'

"But it has marked us brown-tails for mistreatment.

'That is not what should have ever happened. Thus I need you to let My people know the truth, that all are created equal. Just as I love all my precious horse-people, every horse-person should love all other horse-persons, regardless of who anyone happens to be in love with. That is the message I need you to tell My people. And I gave science the ability to prove the truth of My message. 'Now you must go back and tell them.'

"With that, I heard the voice of an angel. At least the voice sounded like an angel, and I found myself back in my own body. I opened my eyes, and there was Ty. Then I realized that my throat hurt, and I couldn't speak. So they got me some paper, and I began to write. And did I ever write! But this is the message that is most important, and I just had to deliver it as soon as possible. I don't know if or how many will believe me. But that's what happened. I swear."

The crowd was silent as Joey left the podium. But when the professor stepped up to speak, the crowd broke out with all sorts of questions. It took a while before the crowd calmed down enough for his words to be heard, but eventually he began to speak.

"Mares and stallions, science cannot verify what Joey Quarterhorse said he experienced because there is no way of proving or disproving it. With science, we only deal with things that can be proven. Religion should limit itself to those things that cannot be proven. Otherwise religious leaders risk possibly misleading the public. Or worse, making religion a false belief.

"In the case of brown-tails, science has finally verified beyond a shadow of a doubt that their existence is a naturally occurring, spontaneously generated happenstance. It has been observed and documented as occurring in virtually every sexual species that has been observed for any length of time, and our species is no exception. Traditional religious beliefs are wrong here as it is *not* a choice. A certain percentage of the male population will be brown-tails, and there is nothing that either they or we can do about it. We cannot predict who will be a brown-tail. Nor can we change a brown-tail into a white-tail. It is similar to the spontaneous generation of being left side oriented. So as far as science is concerned, there is neither a logical nor justifiable reason that a brown-tail should be treated any differently than a white-tail.

"As a scientist as well as a caring horse-person, I can no longer tolerate the traditional religious belief that condemns brown-tails, or that sanctions or enables their historic mistreatment. I must speak out. What Joey Quarterhorse managed to survive, an attempted murder, is unprecedented in our horse-people society. We are a gentle, caring species. But now we have to deal with a violent crime and a religious crisis of moral beliefs. In this one incident, we have a crisis that is going to force major changes in our society."

With that said, the group left the podium area, with Joey and Tyler in the lead. The room was left in chaos. The press corps hurriedly filed their stories, while members of the public were left talking among themselves.

CHAPTER 22

The World Changes

News of Joey's revelation hit the government theocrats with devastating results. Not only had the entire Board of Elders been forced into hiding by the attack on him, clergy worldwide also retreated to their homes, and most had not been seen since. The first message the Elders sent out had been buried as the press followed the public's interest in Joey's story. And each part of his and Tyler's stories fired even more interest. Joey's statement had been the final and most devastating blow to the theocracy and sent even the most religious of horse-people reeling. The scientist's statement just sealed the deal.

Meanwhile, all Joey and Tyler wanted was to be left alone. The whole experience had bonded them in their relationship, and they were now inseparable. During Joey's hospital stay, the staff had set up a bed for Tyler. They had even managed to lash the two frames together, so the two studs could snuggle and sleep together. The physical cuddling Ty gave Joey helped speed his recovery.

Mail and other communications from around the world piled up during Joey's recovery. Kyle Whitehorse, Andy Thoroughbred, and Jennifer Trotter all volunteered to help sort and read all the mail and inquiries. And though they had plenty of classmates who joined them, the task was daunting.

The unspeakable violence of the crime had so stunned the entire world that everyone's attention was focused on the brown-tail couple and what the so-called traditional theological views had wrought. It caused a wholesale epiphany about how hypocritical their religious views were to their ingrained gentle natures. The timeliness of the latest scientific discoveries solidified public opinion solidly behind the brown-tail community.

There suddenly seemed to be brown-tails all over. One after another bravely let others know of their tail color. And once told, most of their friends, families, and acquaintances realized just how wrong their religious teachings had been. Brown-tails weren't any different than white-tails after all. They were just attracted to each other and posed no problems to anyone else.

This sudden realization also adversely affected those with strong religious beliefs. Their world was now turned upside down. Their confidence in their religious beliefs was broken and their leaders nowhere to be found. With no guidance, they were left floundering, with nowhere to turn. Even the Morality Police squads fell apart, and the gates of the Correction Camp were left unlocked and open.

The entire theocracy, from the Board of Elders down, was coming apart at the seams. Their authority over the society was shattered and crumbling. But the public's faith in their spiritual God took a leap, just not in the direction of the traditional leaders. Rather, their faith now was in what Joey had said in his statement to the press and everything he and Ty wrote right after he awoke from the coma.

The letters and other communications arriving at the hospital were overwhelmingly positive. A growing percentage came from the moderately religious types who always had questions about the traditional prohibitions that had been preached against brown-tails.

But the biggest news broke the day Joey was to be released from the hospital. A public opinion poll had been taken, and the results were startling. The public now had a favorable view of brown-tails and little faith in traditional religious teachings. Horse-people were ready to adopt a new religion. And they were about to get just what they needed.

The poll's results were issued just minutes before Ty wheeled Joey to the door. Kyle Whitehorse met them but had to wade through the crowd. Hospital security was pressed to the limit, but the couple made it safely into the car. The press clamored for any word from Joey, but all he had to say was, "No comment." What he had planned would come soon enough.

CHAPTER 23

Joey's Testament

When Joey released what he had written, it would revolutionize religion and the entire world government. Released to the internet, it began by repeating his initial statement in full. But the new statement elaborated on it by adding:

> These are the exact words that were spoken to me and what happened to me when I died as a result of being hanged by a rope around my neck, strung up from a tree, and left to strangle to death. I was instructed to write down every word spoken.
>
> As I mentioned previously, I met the Great One, whose splendor radiated from Him like light from the sun, but it was infinitely more brilliant. I could feel His love wash through me as light shines through glass, and it warmed every particle of my being. He addressed me by name and then motioned me to come to Him and sit down on the grass. Then He instructed me to tell everyone a lot of important things.
>
> Again as I previously said, He began by saying, "Joey Quarterhorse, my dear colt. Much as I love you, it is not your time to be here. But I brought you here for a reason. You are much loved and favored

by Me, and I need someone to tell My beloved horse-people that enough is enough. I have chosen you to tell them that everyone is to be respected and cared for as equally loved horse-people."

I asked, "But why me, oh Great One?"

He explained to me, saying, "I chose you because you have been so true and loyal to Me."

I told him, "Then You know that I love You, Great One?"

"Yes, and I love you, My precious colt."

"But who will listen to me?"

"They will. Trust Me."

"You know I do," I answered.

"Yes. And you will be given the opportunity to address My people. I need you to remind them that I made every horse-person and gave everyone the desire to love another horse-person, regardless of what gender the other horse-person happens to be. I made everyone different—some slightly so, some greatly so. Even identical twins are different from each other because I love diversity. It's diversity that makes a species strong and adaptable.

"I created your world, Equus, and many others like it in the universe. Until now, I have told none of these worlds about the others, but it is time to do so. I populated each one with a different dominate species so that their inherent characteristics may be fully developed. One of My creative tools is what your scientists call evolution, and since time means nothing to Me, I used it over many millions of your years to create and evolve your species as the dominate creatures of Equus. Horses are gentle by nature, so I created your world and evolved horses into horse-people in order to fully develop your gentle nature.

"I have made all these worlds different and every creature, being, and living thing on each world different from each other because I am so complex and need everyone to keep Me occupied. I love all of them, every single thing and every individual of every species on every planet. On each world I am known by a different name. I am known as God, the Lord, Jehovah, Allah, the Supreme Being, and many others. To each species, I appear as one of their own so that they will recognize Me. That is why I will always appear before you and other horse-persons as a horse-person, and just for you, My tail is brown. That is because I love you and will always appear unto you in this form.

"I decided to create a great amount of diversity in horse-people with all manner of markings and physical builds, from sleek quarter horses and colorful palominos to athletic thoroughbreds and muscular Clydesdales, and all with white tails. I was pleased how well all horse-people were at first tolerant of one another. Thus to create even more diversity, I made some studs to be attracted to another of the same sex, just as I had done with all other sexual species, and gave them a brown tail. Yet some have misinterpreted My words and used them to justify their hidden intolerances.

"I gave each world I created My instructions—what you call scriptures—on how to treat each other. They tell the same story of life and of My existence so that those populating the world would not feel alone and unguided. The scriptures form the basis for each of those worlds' religions. The stories and parables in the scriptures help answer what they cannot understand or what cannot be explained or proven. It is why their belief in the scriptures is called faith.

"I then gave the people on each world the logic and rationality of science in order to deal only with what can be proven while remaining silent on matters that cannot be proven. It is when faith tries to dictate what science can explain that faith can go astray. Faith must always bow to science or risk being proven wrong. It is what you could call the 'flat Equus effect.' If a religion were to claim that Equus was flat and then science prove that it was round, that religion would have to change its doctrine or be laughed into the dustbin of history.

"I left evidence of My handiwork all over each world so scientists on those worlds would find that evidence. Some planets' people have discovered these truths on their own. But some, like yours, have not or have chosen to deny the obvious. I have chosen you as My messenger to denounce them as heretics and to tell them these truths.

"In the scriptures, I often used parables as believable stories to explain what they could not otherwise understand. For example, the story of the first two horse-people, a stallion and a mare, is just such a parable, and the pasture of Eden is symbolic. I allowed many mistakes and contradictions to be made in the various scriptures in order to let horse-people know that the scriptures are not to be taken literally, word for word. Rather, they are to be taken as riddles to be contemplated upon as I put the truth behind the words and deep in the meanings of the stories. The book of scriptures is a guidebook, not a rulebook.

"I gifted some with the talent for making money with the intention that they use their excess wealth to benefit society and those less fortunate. I gave others various other talents and what is known as 'luck' to be used to the benefit of those without such talents and abilities. I will deal harshly with those who use their gifts selfishly. And as for those who would deceive others, who would take advantage of the defenseless, or harm those who are already in difficulties, I will make them regret their sinful acts.

"I added a warning for no one to judge anyone as I am the Supreme Judge of all. Those who would set themselves up in My place will be judged by Me as they have judged others. Woe be it to those who would misinterpret the scriptures just so they could justify their own judging of others who are different. I also have ruled out anyone condemning others, as that would require them to pass judgment on others. I told them in the scriptures that none are in any condition to tell others they are condemned. Woe to those who, by their own condemnations, enable others to mistreat those who are different just because they regard them as sinners. That is heresy, and they are heretics for all have sinned against Me.

"I also put cautionary words in the scriptures about those who abused others by misusing themselves in ways that were not their natures. Yet some who claim they speak for Me have misinterpreted those passages and used them against My beloved brown-tails. Woe be it especially to those who so mistreat my precious brown-tails for being different for whatever they have done to them, they have done to Me. Thus I will deal with them most severely of all.

"I alone will be the judge of sin while forgiving those who repent of their transgressions, whether against Me or against others. Love and tolerance should be all that matters to those who are loyal to Me.

"You have heard those who say that they love the sinner but hate the sin. That is blasphemy for that is not possible for mortals to do. Only I am capable of loving the sinner and hating the sin. If a mere mortal tries that, the result will be like trying to serve two masters."

"And I know how that turns out, oh Great One," I exclaimed.

"Exactly, My beloved colt," He answered. "You know your scriptures. In every verse and story, the key is just two simple things: love Me, and love one another unconditionally. But woe be it to those who do not heed these words, who condemn others, or empower others to do wrong against others. I will deal with them accordingly.

"Tell my beloved horse-people to just treat others with the love and respect due all My creations and to have compassion for those in misery. I intended every civilization to be caretakers of their planets and guardians of everyone and everything on it, living or not. Woe be it to those who are not good stewards of that of which I have bestowed on them. Woe be the society that doesn't take care of the very young, the very old, and the helpless. They would not be civilized unless they did.

"But blessed are those who are different because diversity gives a species adaptability and strength. I created most individuals in each sexual species to be attracted to the opposite sex so that the species will thrive. But to add interest in the species, I made a certain percentage to be attracted to their own sex. This your scientists have observed in nature and documented it. You are a brown-tail because I wanted you to be so. And you have pleased Me well in your attraction to Tyler."

I responded with, "He is a beautiful stud, oh Great One. And so kind and gentle. I can't not love him."

"Then your pairing pleases Me" the Great One continued. "But it is unfortunate that some mistreated you two. And as I have said, for whatever they've done to you I will regard as though they had done it to Me. They will be dealt with as suits their wickedness. Woe be it to those who would treat others in any way that is not a loving manner.

"I created all these worlds and every creature and being on them with the ability to love others of their own kind, and even other creatures of their worlds. Love, love is the most important thing to Me. It matters not who loves whom as long as they love another horse-person. Even gender does not matter, just as I created you for Tyler, and he for you."

"But did You have to give us different colored tails?" I asked.

He answered my question by saying, "I thought that would make it obvious that just as you cannot change the color of your tail, you cannot change the orientation of your sexual nature. Nor can a tiger change its stripes or a leopard change its spots. I gave everyone their sexual desires before they were born, but your religious leaders have misinterpreted those wishes that I expressed in the scriptures and have persisted in using them to justify their own prejudices and hatreds. So I have had to give your scientists more proof and even shock everyone with the violence that you have experienced.

"But love is love, and because I created both males and females, I love both genders equally. So to those who would love someone of the opposite gender, I gave them a white tail, and to those who would love someone of their own gender, I gave them a brown tail. Thusly marked, they would more easily be able to find each other. Your tail is brown so that you and Tyler could find one another more easily. Others should not have mistreated you two."

"But they did."

"That was their own choice. Thus I need you to let My horse-people know the truth, that all are created equal. Because I love all My precious horse-people, every horse-person should respect all other horse-people, regardless of whomever anyone happens to be in love with, and treat one another with love. That is the message I need you to tell My horse-people."

"But aren't these all things that your Great Savior told us about in the scriptures?" I asked. "Why do you need me to say what He said? And why would anyone listen to me? I am just an ordinary teenager, nothing special."

"Yes, I laid all these things out in the scriptures already," the Great One said. "But you *are* special. Special to Me because you are you. And by writing all this down, everyone will know that I sent you. Did I not once tell My followers through Him that by the fruit of one's labors, they would know You and who sent You?

"Yet today there are those who have not followed My scriptures but misused them to back up their own hatreds. Look what they did to you and Tyler. That kind of treatment terrified My precious Jamie Colter so much that when his tail grew out brown, he killed himself. It wasn't his time to be here, but he didn't want to return. It broke My heart so much that I kept him here because I love all My precious horse-people, white-tails and brown-tails alike.

"But what happened to you has finally shocked everyone and opened their minds to be told these lessons again, that I only expect everyone to love and respect one another. Because of what happened to you, the people will listen to you. And the scientists will be able to prove the truth of this message to back you up.

"I created you for Tyler and he for you so that neither of you would be alone or unloved in your worldly existence. And he is waiting for your return. Now you must go back and tell them."

With that, I found myself being drawn back through the tunnel of light by the sweet voice of

my beloved stud-friend, Tyler. His was the first face
I saw when I opened my eyes, and my heart leaped
for joy. I knew then that our same-sex relationship
was indeed blessed by the Great One.

These are His words, and I have written them
down just as He instructed me to do. His message
for everyone is that only love matters. Amen.

Joey and Tyler had become instantly famous since horse-people
were naturally drawn to the peaceful of their species. The horror
of the crime that befell them only served to bolster an underlying
feeling of sympathy from a surprising majority for the brown-tails.
And Joey's message from the Great One about love for all regardless
of tail color made them the toast of the entire world.

CHAPTER 24

~~~~~~~~~~~~~~~~

Reconciliation!

Joey and Tyler were now recognized wherever they went. And they didn't have to hide their tails anymore because there seemed to be at least one brown-tail out everywhere they went. Almost everyone treated them well. Sure, there were those old-school religious die-hards, but they had come to the realization that they were in the minority now, and their attitudes weren't very welcome anymore. Many were even rethinking those ideas and slowly coming around. But what surprised the young stud couple the most were Ty's parents.

Ty's mom was the first to reach out to her son. The phone rang one evening, and Ty answered it.

"Ty," she began, "it's your mom."

Tyler almost dropped the phone. "Mom," was all he could manage to choke out.

"I'm sorry for everything," she said. "Your dad and I have been rethinking everything—our religious views, the horrible way we treated you, everything. Your dad especially feels bad for how he threw out his only son with nothing at all. We want to see you again to say we're sorry."

"Mom, I've missed you and Dad," Ty whimpered back.

"And we've missed you too, Ty. Can you forgive us?"

Tears flowed down Ty's face. "You don't have to ask."

"Can we meet you and your stud-friend?" she choked out.

"I, uh, we'd love to. Name the place and time." Ty was almost bawling like a newborn colt by now. His mom told him when and where, and he agreed. Then he slowly hung up the phone.

Joey had come into the room, and seeing him in tears, quickly took Ty in his arms. "What's wrong, honey?" he asked. It was all Ty could do to choke out details of the phone call between sobs.

"I've wanted to reconcile with my folks for so long, and now they want to see me. Us, actually. I can't believe it. It's like I'm dreaming."

"But it is real, honey. And that's fantastic news!" Joey nuzzled Ty affectionately.

"Yes. I just hope they're ready to see me with you. You know, holding hands, nuzzling, being our usual affectionate selves."

"Look, if they have come this far to call you, they're already to the point where they can handle seeing two stud horses madly in love with each other. Trust me."

"I just hope so. They were always a bit prudish in case you didn't know."

"They threw you out of your own house, didn't they? Of course, they were prudish and old school. But it sounds like they've made great strides and have had a sincere change of heart. Give them a chance."

"OK. But I'll still be a bit nervous about showing my affection to you in front of them."

"Understood. But it'll be OK," Joey replied. "Now let's get together with them and see." Joey kissed Tyler affectionately and tightened his arms around him. Making their way to their stall, they bedded down for the evening. Before long, they wrapped their arms around each other and snuggled tightly together. Ty nuzzled Joey, and he nuzzled back. Then they both drifted off to a deep, comfortable sleep.

The day of the meeting with Ty's parents, Joey was as nervous as a young colt on the first day of school. But Tyler was even more nervous. Ty hadn't seen his parents since they had thrown him out so long ago. They were so hostile about his tail color back then. But now they were about to meet his stud-friend. The difference was not just big, it was going to be monumental. And not just for the stud-couple. It would be quit a leap for Ty's parents. After living with their learned prejudice all their lives, they were now faced with a total reversal of everything they had ever thought about brown-tails.

But there they were. Mom and Dad Palomino rang the doorbell of the Whitehorse home, where Ty and Joey shared the spare room. Mrs. Whitehorse answered the door and invited them in. Mr. Whitehorse escorted them to the living room and then went down the hall to Ty and Joey's room. The two studs slowly came out, one after the other, and entered the living room. Then the tears began to flow, first with Mrs. Palomino and then with Ty. The two threw their arms around each other and cried.

"I'm so sorry, Ty," Mom sobbed.

"I'm OK, Mom," Ty said softy.

Then Mr. Palomino threw his arms around the two. "Can you ever forgive me, son?" was all he could choke out.

"Mom, Dad, I know. And it's OK. I'm doing OK now." They all hugged.

"Mom, Dad." Tyler pulled away a little and reached out for Joey. "This is Joey, my stud-friend. I love him, and he loves me. I don't expect you to—"

"Son," his dad interrupted, "we know. At first it was hard to accept, but your mom and I have given it a lot of thought. And now we're just glad you have someone to love you. We never really stopped loving you either. It's just that—"

It was Ty's turn to interrupt. "I know, Dad. You don't have to explain. I just want you two to get acquainted with him."

Ty pulled Joey next to him. "Son, as long as you two love each other, I'm sure we'll all get acquainted with one another," Dad said.

Ty nuzzled Joey as his parents put their arms around the two studs.

The Whitehorses stood by and smiled. The reunion was a success.

CHAPTER 25

The New Order

As soon as Joey' testament was released on the internet, it hit the religious community even harder than his initial statement had done. The traditionalists' religious leaders had silently hunkered down behind closed doors, leaving their most devoted followers speechless and at a loss. With their first response being inadequate, not to mention being buried by news from the hospital, and no further word of explanation from the Board of Elders, the rest of the clergy were reluctant to say anything in case they would be later contradicted by the elders.

So the Board of Elders were forced to respond again. But how? The violence of the crime had ripped the façade from their traditional teachings, and the fact that it had been committed by the sons of one of their own had exposed the hypocrisy of their dogma. And Elder Joe's suicide was the final proof of its fallacy. Obviously they were going to have to renounce their previous teachings against brown-tails or face being laughed into oblivion. So at their hastily called emergency meeting, one could almost hear their theocratic government crumbling as many of the elders were confused and shocked, which left the meeting in disarray.

Finally, Elder Ralph offered to write up a yet another response. Elder John volunteered to help him. They went off by themselves and returned shortly with a statement. The rest of the elders on the board read it and quickly agreed. It was then posted on the internet to the world. But would it be too late? The public quickly decided.

It seemed that no matter what the bulletins the Board of Elders put out, fewer and fewer horse-people were paying attention to them. The board's power over the public was shattered, and their theocratic government was now irrelevant. The incidents surrounding the attempted murder of Joey by Elder Joe Clydesdale's sons and the elder's subsequent suicide had so completely shocked everyone that only a completely new beginning was possible, and necessary. And it was Joey who was going to give the world a new start. The public clamored for him to make more of his story known, so the media pressed him to give another news conference. But this was all he said:

> Everyone, this is my last statement. I have released the manuscript I wrote after I awoke from the coma, and that will be all that is necessary, now and in the future. I am asking everyone to leave me and my family alone and to refer to my manuscript from here on. Thank you all for your interest and concern, but I'm sure the Great One would want us to have our lives to ourselves. So with that said, I will say goodbye.

Joey left the press microphone, retired into the house, and closed the front door.

There was a rush to read Joey's manuscript on the internet. It quickly became the new scripture and the founding document for a new government based on science and theology sharing their respective authorities over provable and unprovable doctrines. The new religion sprang up to fill the void left by the collapse of the old. But now, all horse-people were equally respected.

Tyler and Joey eventually graduated from school, got married, and happily lived the rest of their lives together. But that's another tail.

JOEY'S TESTAMENT

Joey Quarterhorse

Translated to human by Mark Rogers

These are the exact words spoken to me and what happened to me after I died as a result of being hanged by a rope around my neck, strung up a tree, and left to strangle to death. I was instructed to write down everything and every word spoken.

I remember that as I gasped for air and lost consciousness, I found myself in a tunnel of light, traveling at a full sprint toward the brightest light I've ever seen. As I came out of the tunnel, I burst into a wide-open field, brightly illuminated that seemed to come from everywhere. The air was fresh and sweet, and I could take in a deep breath for the first time since that rope had tightened around my neck. Everything seemed to be singing, and the sounds were the most beautiful that I have ever heard. It was glorious!

The first person to greet me was a winged angel. "I am Michael, the Lord's chief angel and guardian to the gates of heaven. Welcome, Joey Quarterhorse, into the perfect, eternal world of the one true God."

As I looked around, I saw other people around the field. Some I didn't recognize, while others I did were all men and women who had passed on. Then I saw Jamie Colter waving at me. He was overjoyed at seeing me and came sprinting up to me. I was thrilled to see him, and we hugged. He told me that he made a mistake in hanging himself, that he was supposed to live out his life instead of harming himself. He had done so because his parents were so religious and would have hated him for being gay. He felt that hanging himself was his only way out. But the Lord told him that they were wrong, because He had intentionally made him gay. And because He loved him so much, He brought him to heaven so that he could be close to Him and know he would never feel unloved again. I could tell that Jamie was much loved. He was so happy!

But what came next was a surprise. I was approached by the most majestic pure-white being I had ever seen. He was pure-white from head to foot. His splendor radiated from Him like light from the sun but was infinitely more brilliant. I could feel His love wash through me as light shines through glass, and that warmed every particle of my being. He looked at me and smiled, and I instantly knew exactly who He was. He was the Lord God. He addressed me by name and then motioned for me to come to Him and sit down on the grass. Then He instructed me to tell everyone a lot of important things.

He began by saying "Joey Quarterhorse, My dear boy. Much as I love you, it is not your time to be here. But I brought you here for a reason. You are much loved and favored by Me, and I need someone to tell My beloved human people that enough is enough. I have chosen you as My messenger to denounce those who are heretics and to tell them these truths: All are to be respected and cared for as equally loved human people."

I asked, "But why me, oh Lord?"

He explained to me, saying, "I chose you because you have been so true and loyal to Me."

"Then You know that I love You, Lord."

"Yes, and I love you, My precious son."

"But who will listen to me?"

"They will. Trust Me."

"You know I do."

"Yes. And you will be given the opportunity to address My people. I need you to remind them that I made every person and gave everyone the desire to love another person, regardless of what gender that other person happens to be. I made everyone different—some slightly so, some greatly so. Even identical twins are different from each other because I love diversity. It's diversity that makes a species strong and adaptable.

"I created your world, Earth, and many others like it in the universe. Until now, I have told none of these worlds about the others, but it is time to do so. I populated each one with a different dominate species so that their inherent characteristics may be fully developed. One of My creative tools is what your scientists call evolution, and since time means nothing to Me, I used it over many millions of your years to create and evolve your species as the dominate creatures of Earth. Primates are adaptable by nature, so I created your world and evolved some primates into humans in order to fully develop your adaptable natures.

"I made all these worlds different, and every creature, being, and living thing on each world different from one another because I am so complex, and need everyone to keep Me occupied. I love all of them, every single thing and every individual of every species on every planet. On each world, I am known by a different name. I am known as the Great One, God, the Lord, Jehovah, Allah, the Supreme Being, and many others. To each species, I appear as one of their own so that they will recognize Me. That is why I will always appear before you and other humans as a human person, and just for you, I am gay. That is because I love you and will always appear unto you in this form.

"I decided to create a great amount of diversity in humans with all manner of skin colors and physical builds, from lightly colored Asians to colorful Polynesians, black Africans to white Caucasians, and all straight. I was pleased by how well all humans were at first tolerant of one another. Thus to create even more diversity, I made some humans to be attracted to another of the same sex, just as I had done with all the other sexual species. Yet some have misinterpreted My words and used them to justify their hidden intolerances.

"I gave each world I created my instructions, what you call scriptures, on how to treat one another. They tell the same story of life and of My existence so those populating Earth's various lands would not feel alone and unguided. The scriptures form the basis for each of those worlds' religions. The stories and parables in the scriptures help answer what they cannot understand or what cannot be explained or proven. It is why their belief in the scriptures is called faith.

"I then gave the people on each world the logic and rationality of science in order to deal only with that which can be proven while remaining silent on matters that cannot be proven. It is when faith tries to dictate what science can explain that faith can go astray. Faith must always bow to science or risk being proven wrong. It is what you could call the 'flat Earth effect.' If a religion were to claim that Earth was flat and then science prove that it was round, then that religion would have to change its doctrine or be laughed out of history.

"I left evidence of My evolution handiwork all over each world so that the scientists on those worlds would find that evidence.

Some planets' people have discovered these truths on their own. But some, like yours, have not or have chosen to deny the obvious. I have chosen you as My messenger to denounce them as heretics and to tell them these truths.

"In the scriptures, I often used parables as believable stories to explain what they could not otherwise understand. For example, the story in the Bible of the first two humans, Adam and Eve, is just such a parable, and the Garden of Eden is symbolic. I allowed many mistakes and contradictions to be made in the various books in the Bible in order to let people know that the Bible is not to be taken literally, word for word. But rather, as riddles to be contemplated on as I put the truth behind the words and deep in the meanings of the stories. All scriptures—such as the Bible, Torah, and Koran—are guidebooks, not rulebooks.

"I gifted some with the talent for making money, the Midas touch, with the intention that they use their excess wealth to benefit society and those less fortunate. I gave others various other talents and what is known as 'luck' to be used to the benefit of those without such talents and abilities. I will deal harshly with those who use their gifts selfishly. And as for those who would deceive others, who would take advantage of the defenseless, or harm those who are already in difficulties, I will make them regret their sinful acts.

"I added a warning for no one to judge anyone as I am the Supreme Judge of all. Those who would set themselves up in My place will be judged by Me as they have judged others. Woe be it to those who would misinterpret the scriptures just so they could justify their own judging of others who are different. I also ruled out anyone condemning others, as that would require them to pass judgment on others. I told them in the scriptures that none are in any condition to tell others that they are condemned. Woe to those who by their own condemnations enable others to mistreat those who are different just because they regard them as sinners. That is heresy, and they are heretics for all have sinned against Me.

"I also put cautionary words in the scriptures about those who abuse others by misusing themselves in ways that were not their nature. Yet some who claim that they speak for Me have misinterpreted those passages and used them against My beloved gays. Woe be it especially to those who so mistreat My precious gays for being different for whatever they have done to them, they have done to Me. Thus I will deal with them most severely of all.

"I alone will be the judge of sin, while forgiving those who repent of their transgressions, whether against Me or against others. Love and tolerance should be all that matters to those who are loyal to Me.

"You have heard those who say that they love the sinner but hate the sin. That is blasphemy for that is not possible for mortals to do. Only I am capable of loving the sinner and hating the sin. If a mere mortal tries that, the result will be like trying to serve two masters."

"And I know how that turns out, oh, Lord!" I exclaimed.

"Exactly, my beloved child," He answered. "You know your scriptures.

"In every verse and story, the key is just two simple things: love me, and love one another unconditionally. But woe be it to those who do not heed these words, who condemn others or empower others to do wrong against others as I will deal with them accordingly.

"Tell My beloved people to just treat others with the love and respect due all My creations and to have compassion for those in misery. I intended every civilization to be caretakers of their planets and guardians of everyone and everything on it, living or not. Woe be it to those who are not good stewards of that which I have bestowed on them. Woe be to the society that doesn't take care of the very young, the very old, and the helpless. They would not be civilized unless they did.

"But blessed are those who are different because diversity gives a species adaptability and strength. I created most individuals in each sexual species to be attracted to the opposite sex so that the species will thrive. But to add interest in the species, I made a certain percentage to be attracted to their own sex. This your scientists have observed and documented in nature. You are same-sex-oriented because I wanted you to be so, and you have pleased Me well in your attraction to Tyler."

I responded with, "He is a beautiful guy, oh, Lord. And so kind and gentle. I can't not love him."

"Then your pairing pleases me," the Lord God continued. "But it is unfortunate that some mistreated you two. And as I have said, for whatever they've done to you, I will regard as though they had done it to Me. They will be dealt with as suits their wickedness. Woe be it to those who would treat others in any way that is not a loving manner.

"I created all these various worlds and every creature and being on them with the ability to love others of their own kind, and even other creatures of their world. Love, love is the most important thing to Me. It matters not who loves whom as long as they love another person. Even gender does not matter, just as I created you for Tyler, and he for you."

"But did you have to make us different?" I asked.

He answered my question by saying, "I thought that would make it obvious that just as you cannot change, say the color of your hair, you cannot change the orientation of your sexual nature. Nor can a tiger change its stripes or a leopard change its spots. I gave everyone their sexual desires before they were born, but your religious leaders have misinterpreted the wishes I expressed in the scriptures. They have persisted in using them to justify their own prejudices and hatreds. So I have had to give your scientists more proof and even shock everyone with the violence that you have experienced.

"But love is love, and because I created both males and females, I love both genders equally. So to those who would love someone of the opposite gender, I gave them that preference, and to those who would love someone of their own gender, I gave them that preference. Thus they would more easily be able to find each other. Your attraction to other males shows so that you and Tyler could find each other more easily. Others should not have mistreated you two."

"But they did."

"That was their own choice. Thus I need you to let My people know the truth, that all are created equal. Because I love all My precious people, every person should respect all other people, regardless of who anyone happens to be in love with, and treat one another with love. That is the message I need you to tell My people."

"But aren't these all things that Jesus told us about in the scriptures?" I asked. "Why do You need me to say what He said? And why would anyone listen to me? I am just an ordinary teenager, nothing special."

"Yes, I laid all these things out in the scriptures," the Lord said. "But you *are* special. Special to Me because you are you. And by writing all this down, everyone will know that I sent you. Did I not once tell My followers through Jesus that by the fruit of one's labors they would know you and who sent you?

"Yet today there are those who have not followed My scriptures but misused them to back up their own hatreds. Look what they did to you and Tyler. That kind of treatment was what terrified My precious Jamie Colter so much that when he realized he was gay, he killed himself. It wasn't his time to be here, but he didn't want to return. It broke My heart so much that I kept him here because I love all My precious people, straight or nonstraight alike.

"But what happened to you has finally shocked everyone and opened their minds to be told these lessons again, that I only expect everyone to love and respect one another. Because of what happened to you, the people will listen to you. And the scientists will be able to prove the truth of this message to back you up.

"I created you for Tyler, and he for you so neither of you would be alone or unloved in your worldly existence. And he is waiting for your return. Now you must go back and tell them."

With that I found myself being drawn back through the tunnel of light by the sweet voice of my beloved boyfriend, Tyler. His was the first face I saw when I opened my eyes, and my heart leaped for joy. I knew then that our same-sex relationship was indeed blessed by the Lord God.

These are His words, and I have written them down just as He instructed me to do. His message for everyone is that only love matters. Amen.

AUTHOR'S PERSONAL
NOTES ABOUT THE BIBLE

So many people self-identify as Christian when, in fact, there are many religions that use the Bible, and all commonly go under the label "Christian." What Jesus taught is your basic Christianity, known as "Red-Letter Christianity." All others, often referred to as "denominations," are elaborations on that basic Christianity. Sad to say, some people hold to doctrines that are far removed from what Jesus actually said and did. They use other verses in the Bible to back up thoughts, doctrines, interpretations, and practices that Jesus never said, did, or even indicated His thoughts about the subject. They are, if I may coin a term, "Biblicans," not real Christians.

Scientists have observed and documented same-sex attractions and behavior in virtually every sexual species that has ever been observed for any length of time, as examined in the book "*Biological Exuberance.*"9 The sex to which someone is attracted is spontaneously generated by nature, and therefore not a choice. Since by definition a sin is to willfully choose to rebel against God, to be gay cannot be sinful. Further, a thorough study in a Red-Letter Bible (KJV is used herein) proves that Jesus never said a word about, let alone against, same-sex attraction. Yet by comparison, He roundly criticized divorce except in case of fornication (Matthew 5:31–32). If same-sex attraction was the horrible sin that some self-described Christians claim, you'd think He would have said something about it, but He didn't. So I can only conclude that Jesus recognized that it was not and cannot be a sin. The Bible thus proves that Jesus was not homophobic but quite the opposite. So for a true Christian, homophobia is—or should be—a foreign concept. Those verses in the Bible that are used against the gay community are thus being misinterpreted.

Therefore, all forms of Christianity that promote ideas not mentioned by Jesus are committing heresy. That's the way I think Jesus would see it. And it's high time true Christians call them out as being heretics.

There is also evidence that He saw no difference between a loving same-sex relationship and a loving opposite-sex one. Witness the story of the Roman centurion. Recorded twice in the Bible, the centurion came to Jesus and told Jesus that his *pais* was deathly ill. When properly interpreted, the term translates as the centurion's male lover. And Jesus healed him without batting an eye, even though He knew of their love relationship. (See Matthew 8:5–13 and Luke 7:1–10.)

Jesus was once asked what the greatest commandment of all was, to which He replied, "Love God with all your heart, mind, and soul." Then He surprised everyone by saying, "The second is liken unto it. Love your neighbor as yourself. On these two are based all the laws and rules of the prophets." He was later asked who constituted our neighbor. He responded by telling the story of the Good Samaritan. In other words, our neighbor is anyone we happen to meet while traveling down life's highway. Clearly Jesus meant that even the laws and rules laid down by the prophets are based on treating everyone with respect and love.

He didn't even condemn the woman accused of adultery who was about to be stoned. Jesus dispersed the angry crowd by telling them, "Let he that is without sin, let him cast the first stone." To condemn requires judgment, and He told us not to judge lest we ourselves be judged. Homophobia violates both.

A true Christian should believe that Jesus's direct words take precedence over anything in the Bible written by anyone other than Him. Even then, what is written can sometimes be subject to misinterpretation and bad translation by mortal humans. Therefore, in order to be considered as God's true laws, nothing can contradict what Jesus said. Otherwise, God would be hypocritical. Thus it is clear that we mere mortals are to say and do everything in the true context of loving God and loving everyone else. Regardless of how we read or interpret anything else in the Bible, it must pass that test of truth. Homophobia does not.

The oldest commonly used Bible, the King James Version (KJV), is but five hundred years old and translated from older texts, while the original Bible, as we know it, was composed by Roman Emperor Constantine's Council of Nicene, and was a collection of many texts by many authors. Thus when reading the Bible, one must know who is talking to whom, about what, and under what circumstance. It is best to even study the texts in their oldest known, original languages to make any kind of valid interpretation.

Because of its origins and various reinterpretations over the centuries, the Bible contains many contradictions and mathematical errors between the various authors, and even within their own works. And like any good authors, some doubtlessly took poetic license with their stories in order to appeal to certain audiences. Many probably never knew of others' existence and created things that never were. Many stories were passed on orally, sometimes for many generations, before they were written down. Their stories are more parable than fact in order to get a message across, and thus are not to be taken literally, word for word as real, verified occurrences. Jesus often spoke in parables just to get His message across, so there's nothing wrong in such fabrications. Even the Genesis story of creation is a parable told by an ignorant author lacking today's scientific evidence of evolution. The intention was to explain what to him was incomprehensible to an even more ignorant audience.

My favorite contradiction occurs between Matthew and Luke in the second chapters of those books. It's commonly called the Christmas story, but where they diverge is in the time line between where Mary and Joseph leave Bethlehem until they arrive in Nazareth. The more closely one reads these two stories, word for word, the more conflicted one can get. But traditional Christianity ignores this and blends the two together as if they didn't conflict. That's because to Jesus's message, such conflicts simply don't matter. And that's just one proof that the Bible cannot be taken literally, word for word. Its contradictions and errors are because of the way it was assembled and from what texts. Thus Jesus told us to "study" the scriptures because He well knew that people would misinterpret them if they merely read them and cherry-picked them for passages they liked while ignoring contradictory facts.

But the truth is, when seriously studied and taken in proper context, there is nothing in the Bible that condemns or even looks down on a loving same-sex relationship. Its verses address only abusive relationships and acts. Instead, the Bible is actually gay-positive. In 2 Samuel 1:23, 26–27, David declares of Jonathan that "your love to me was wonderful, (sur)passing the love of women." This was no "just friends" relationship as it has been glossed over by so many self-proclaimed Christian preachers. No, it was a rip-snorting physical, emotional, and sexual love affair. At their very first meeting, Jonathan strips himself naked and gives David his most prized possessions. That is, by any measure, obviously the beginning of a physical and sexual affair. Just read about their relationship, scattered in verses from 1 Samuel 13 through 2 Samuel 1. There is no mention whatsoever that either they or their relationship found any disfavor from God.

To the contrary. The Bible says of David that he had found the favor of God. So it's no wonder that God raised him to be king, one of the most revered kings in Jewish history. It's recorded that David did eventually marry Saul's younger daughter, Michal, and had a second wife. Yet women at that time were little more than property. In a warlike, patriarchal society, a male not only had to have a male heir in order to keep his material estate in the family, but that male heir had to be old enough to be a capable warrior in order to ascend to the throne. They would have no queens. So even though Jonathan kept wives on the side to provide that critical male heir, he did not have a son who was old enough to ascend the throne. On the deaths of Saul and all his sons, it thus fell on David, a common shepherd boy but a proven warrior, to ascend to the royal throne. I feel it was not because of his marriage to Jonathan's sister but because of his same-sex love relationship to Jonathan, who was King Saul's heir. So David and Jonathan's love is one of the greatest romances of all time, and it's a same-sex relationship recorded in the very book Christians hold most dear! And my Christianity is one of love, not just only for straight humans, but for every human.

It's time for true Christians to denounce those who use the religion they have supposedly derived from the Bible and beat others over the head with it. Those people are heretics, not true Christians!

For further reading and study, there are many good books

available. I recommend, among others, *Rescuing the Bible from Fundamentalism,* by Bishop John Shelby Spong, and *The Children Are Free,* by Rev. Jeff Miner and John Tyler Connoley. There are also many churches and religious organizations (such as the Universal Unitarian Church and the Universal Fellowship of Metropolitan Community Churches) that cite scripture to teach love, equality, and acceptance for all people. The websites http://www.soulforce .org/resources/, https://www.faithfulamerica.org/, and http://www .welcomingresources.org/resources.htm are good online resources as well.

APPENDIX A

About Equus

It has been estimated that there are possibly as many as ten thousand planets in the universe with civilizations like ours. This story is set in one such civilization on Planet Equus. Specifically, it is the tale of one of its inhabitants. To translate their people into terms that we can understand, comparisons must first be made, and their words translated to ours as closely as possible.

Their species is what we'd call horse-people as they are very similar to a cross between Earth's horse and human species. Obviously, they evolved from horses instead of primates like we did. They have only one race. Males generally having a naturally muscular build; females are similar but sleeker in build. All have a skin coated in short, velvet-like hair that varies in color from medium brown to tan, often with white markings specific to each individual. The only long body hair are their manes (and sometimes wrist and ankle hair) and the male adult's tail. Everyone has hoof-like feet and hands with what we'd call two thumbs (one on each side of the palm), opposed by four fingers with strong, thick fingernails. A clenched fist looks like a hoof, while their feet are solid hooves. Their heads are decidedly horse-like, somewhat elongated with a short but prominent, projecting muzzle for the nose and mouth.

Translated, their term for the adult male of their species is "stallion," and the female is a "mare." Male children are called colts and female children ponies. A teen male is a stud, and a teen female is a filly. In our language, we don't have any corresponding terms for teen males and females.

In this world, children don't have tails, but toward the end of puberty, instead of facial hair like us, studs start growing a flowing, normally white tail. A stud's tail grows to knee length within about a year. One hair after another suddenly sprouts from their tailbone area, grows to full length, and then stops growing. Thus no trimming is needed, just regular grooming. Razors, scissors, and other hair-trimming hardware are sometimes used, though, as horse-people love to be well-groomed. Fillies merely grow a spot of short hair over their tailbone area that only grows to about an inch in length. Hence, mares and fillies are sometimes called bobtails.

Males are literally, "hung like a horse." The stallion's genital size is matched in the mare's anatomy, and this large size results in childbirth that is free from the pain that humans experience. Due to their genital size, the accepted male's underwear, worldwide, is the elephant-trunk brief, which sports an integral sleeve just for the penis, allowing it to stand out and hang freely. An opening in the back allows the tail to hang freely out the back; this style is called a tail brief. Colt-size briefs don't have a tail hole, while stud and stallion sizes do. Swimwear also follows this design, but just doesn't have the underwear's opening at the end of the sleeve. Thus stallions are noted for needing a large pouch-like bulge built into the front of their jeans or slacks, with most studs also choosing to have a tail opening as well. Young studs consider the growth of their tails to be the most definitive mark of their masculine coming of age, and prize the occasion when they get their first tail briefs and jeans so that they can show off their tails.

Some items are a little different than what humans are used to seeing or using. Chairs are always open-back or split-back designs so that a male's tail will hang freely out the back, and the male can sit down and move as needed without his tail causing any problems. Even toilets are a little different and used differently than what is found on Earth. A toilet is mounted on the wall with a deep oval bowl and a seat with a split back in the front of the bowl. The user opens his jeans, drops them to the floor, straddles the bowl, and sits down facing the wall. His tail falls into the split in the back and is protected from any accidental dip in the drink.

Females are exclusively opposite-sex oriented. And while most males are also, about 5 percent are exclusively same-sex oriented, which for reasons unknown, always causes their tail hair to grow out brown instead of white.

Their society is similar to ours, but their government is a theocracy, run by the Board of Elders. For several millenniums, theocrats have interpreted their religion's sacred writings to say that same-sex attraction is the result of a conscience decision to rebel against their God, "the Great One," and their theocratic government, and that brown-tails are to be reviled. It is only recently that scientific evidence has begun to challenge those beliefs. Some scientists and archaeologists have theorized that instead of having been created by the Great One in one sudden burst of creation, their race evolved from more primitive horse species, and thus, occasional variations can be expected to occur naturally. The religious hierarchy has retaliated with charges of heresy against those who dare to challenge their centuries-old accepted religious dogma.

APPENDIX B

Notes of Interest

Suicide is the second-leading cause of death among young people ages ten to twenty-four,[1] and one out of six students nationwide considered suicide this past year.[2] Suicide attempts are four times higher for gay, lesbian, and bisexual young people than their straight peers. Nearly half of young transgender people have seriously thought about taking their lives, and one quarter report having made a suicide attempt.[3] But having one supportive person in someone's life reduces the risk of suicide by 30 percent.

Studies find that 40 percent of America's homeless youth are LGBT. Fifty percent of LGBT teens report a negative reaction to coming out, and one in four LGBT teens are thrown out of their homes after coming out. LGB youth who come from highly rejecting families are 8.4 times as likely to have attempted suicide as LGB peers who reported no or low levels of family rejection.[4]

Once on the street, LGBT teens are in a fight for their lives. With nowhere to turn, they are easy targets for physical abuse and sexual exploitation. Roughly 58 percent of homeless gay or trans teens have been sexually victimized.[5] All too often, shelters report LGBT kids appearing with stab wounds, bruises, bullet wounds, and extreme sexual trauma. Each episode of LGBT victimization, such as physical or verbal harassment or abuse, increases the likelihood of self-harming behavior by 2.5 times on average.[6]

Suicide attempts by LGB youth and questioning youth are four to six times more likely to result in injury, poisoning, or overdose that requires treatment from a doctor or nurse, compared to their straight peers.[7] So it should be no surprise that 62 percent of homeless LGBT youth attempt suicide.[8]

REFERENCES

[1]CDC, NCIPC. (2010). Web-based Injury Statistics Query and Reporting System (WISQARS). Accessed August 1, 2013. www.cdc.gov/ncipc/wisqars.

[2]CDC. (2011). Youth Risk Behavior Surveillance—United States, 2011. Atlanta: US Department of Health and Human Services.

[3]Grossman, A. H., and A. R. D'Augelli. (2007). Transgender youth and life-threatening behaviors. *Suicide and Life-Threatening Behaviors*, 37(5), 527–537.

[4]Family Acceptance Project™. (2009). Family rejection as a predictor of negative health outcomes in white and Latino lesbian, gay, and bisexual young *adults*. Pediatrics, 123(1), 346–352.

[5]Information quote taken from an email from the Trevor Project.

[6]IMPACT. (2010). Mental health disorders, psychological distress, and suicidality in a diverse sample of lesbian, gay, bisexual, and transgender youths. *American Journal of Public Health*, 100(12), 2426–2432.

[7]CDC. (2011). *Sexual Identity, Sex of Sexual Contacts, and Health-Risk Behaviors Among Students in Grades 9–12: Youth Risk Behavior Surveillance*. Atlanta: US Department of Health and Human Services.

[8]Information quote taken from an email from the Trevor Project.

[9]Bagemihl, Bruce, PhD, *Biological Exuberance: Animal Homosexuality and Natural Diversity*, St. Martin's Press, New York, 1999.

Tyler has a secret that puts him at odds with his very religious parents and that could destroy his whole life. But the intolerance generated from centuries of scriptural misinterpretations is brought to a raging boil when he falls in love with the right person at just the right time. Will that love destroy the entire world or save it?

This sci-fi romp should make everyone claiming to be Christian question whether they are true to the words of Jesus or just pretending to follow Him. It pulls the covers off the harm religion can do to people under the pretense of love. It shows what true love is and what true Christians should be like.

Printed in the United States
by Baker & Taylor Publisher Services